D0391239

This n
HIGHLY COMPROMISED POSITION
by Sara Orwig

When one night with a stranger ends in pregnancy,
Rose Windcroft is determined to raise her baby
on her own. Too bad the father thinks differently.
Tom Devlin is equally determined to be there
for his child. Their differences are enough to
resurrect the Windcroft-Devlin feud!

SILHOUETTE DESIRE
IS PROUD TO PRESENT

A new drama unfolds for six of the state's
wealthiest bachelors.

* * *

And don't miss the final installments of the
TEXAS CATTLEMAN'S CLUB:
THE SECRET DIARY series

A MOST SHOCKING REVELATION
by Kristi Gold
December 2005

Available from Silhouette Desire!

Dear Reader,

It's November and perhaps the weather is turning a bit cooler where you are…so why not heat things up with six wonderful Silhouette Desire novels? *New York Times* bestselling author Diana Palmer is back this month with a LONG, TALL TEXANS story not to be missed. You've loved Blake Kemp and his ever-faithful assistant, Violet, in other books…. Now you finally get their love story, in *Boss Man*.

Heat continues to generate in DYNASTIES: THE ASHTONS with Laura Wright's contribution, *Savor the Seduction*. Grant and Anna shared a night of passion some months ago…now he's wondering if they have a shot at a repeat performance. And the temperature continues to rise as Sara Orwig delivers her share of surprises, in *Highly Compromised Position*, the latest installment in the TEXAS CATTLEMAN'S CLUB: THE SECRET DIARY series. (Hint, someone in Royal, Texas, is pregnant!)

Brenda Jackson gets things simmering in *The Chase Is On*, another fabulous Westmoreland story with a strong emphasis on food…tasty! And Bronwyn Jameson is back with the conclusion of her PRINCES OF THE OUTBACK series. Who wouldn't want to share body heat with *The Ruthless Groom?* Last but not least, get all hot and bothered in the boardroom with Margaret Allison's business-becomes-pleasure holiday story, *Mistletoe Maneuvers*.

Here's hoping you find plenty of ways to keep yourself warm. Enjoy all we have to offer at Silhouette Desire.

Best,

Melissa Jeglinski

Melissa Jeglinski
Senior Editor
Silhouette Books

Please address questions and book requests to:
Silhouette Reader Service
U.S.: 3010 Walden Ave., P.O. Box 1325, Buffalo, NY 14269
Canadian: P.O. Box 609, Fort Erie, Ont. L2A 5X3

HIGHLY
COMPROMISED
Position

SARA ORWIG

Published by Silhouette Books

America's Publisher of Contemporary Romance

If you purchased this book without a cover you should be aware that this book is stolen property. It was reported as "unsold and destroyed" to the publisher, and neither the author nor the publisher has received any payment for this "stripped book."

Special thanks and acknowledgment are given to Sara Orwig for her contribution to the TEXAS CATTLEMAN'S CLUB: THE SECRET DIARY series.

 SILHOUETTE BOOKS

ISBN 0-373-76689-0

HIGHLY COMPROMISED POSITION

Copyright © 2005 by Harlequin Books S.A.

All rights reserved. Except for use in any review, the reproduction or utilization of this work in whole or in part in any form by any electronic, mechanical or other means, now known or hereafter invented, including xerography, photocopying and recording, or in any information storage or retrieval system, is forbidden without the written permission of the editorial office, Silhouette Books, 233 Broadway, New York, NY 10279 U.S.A.

All characters in this book have no existence outside the imagination of the author and have no relation whatsoever to anyone bearing the same name or names. They are not even distantly inspired by any individual known or unknown to the author, and all incidents are pure invention.

This edition published by arrangement with Harlequin Books S.A.

® and TM are trademarks of Harlequin Books S.A., used under license. Trademarks indicated with ® are registered in the United States Patent and Trademark Office, the Canadian Trade Marks Office and in other countries.

Visit Silhouette Books at www.eHarlequin.com

Printed in U.S.A.

Books by Sara Orwig

Silhouette Desire

Falcon's Lair #938
The Bride's Choice #1019
A Baby for Mommy #1060
Babes in Arms #1094
Her Torrid Temporary Marriage #1125
The Consummate Cowboy #1164
The Cowboy's Seductive Proposal #1192
World's Most Eligible Texan #1346
Cowboy's Secret Child #1368
The Playboy Meets His Match #1438
Cowboy's Special Woman #1449
*Do You Take This Enemy? #1476
*The Rancher, the Baby & the Nanny #1486
Entangled with a Texan #1547
†Shut Up and Kiss Me #1581
†Standing Outside the Fire #1594
Estate Affair #1657
Highly Compromised Position #1689

Silhouette Intimate Moments

Hide in Plain Sight #679
Galahad in Blue Jeans #971
*One Tough Cowboy #1192
†Bring on the Night #1298
†Don't Close Your Eyes #1316

*Stallion Pass
†Stallion Pass: Texas Knights

SARA ORWIG

lives in Oklahoma. She has a patient husband who will take her on research trips anywhere from big cities to old forts. She is an avid collector of Western history books. With a master's degree in English, Sara has written historical romance, mainstream fiction and contemporary romance. Books are beloved treasures that take Sara to magical worlds, and she loves both reading and writing them.

To Cindy, Shirley, Brenda, Michelle and Kristi
with many thanks. Thanks also to Melissa Jeglinski.
It was great to get to work with all of you!

Prologue

From the diary of Jessamine Golden

November 4, 1910

Dear Diary:

On this day my heart is broken.

I think that love means trust. I love Sheriff Brad Webster with all of my being, but he doesn't believe what I'm telling him. He doesn't trust me and he accepts the accusations of others against me instead of considering what I tell him. I'm being honest with him. How it hurts to learn that he takes the words of others over mine.

I know the gold I am accused of stealing was taken by the mayor, Edgar Halifax. He has fooled everyone in this town! Including the sheriff. I'd think your heart would tell you which person to believe.

I'm deeply unhappy now. The stronger my love for Brad grows, the more trouble I get into with the law. There was a poker game recently with fierce stakes. According to the word around town, Nicholas Devlin cheated Richard Windcroft. It's true! I know Nicholas had the mayor's help. Later I tricked Nicholas into admitting his cheating to me. He also told me that he knew Edgar filched the gold and laid the blame for the theft on me.

Nicholas knew the truth. I thought I could get him to reveal it to Brad...Sheriff Webster. My heart pounds just writing his name. How I longed to be Mrs. Brad Webster! My dearest Brad—you will never know how much I love you. My heart belongs to Sheriff Brad Webster who can only see that I have broken the law that he upholds.

My dear diary, my tears are falling on the pages as I write. Nicholas Devlin, my one hope, was murdered. I am certain it was by Edgar's hand, but I have no way to prove who the killer was.

Edgar Halifax—what a wicked, evil man!

Last week I took the gold from Edgar and sent him a note telling him. He can't accuse me twice, can he? My message dared him to confront me.

Mayor Halifax is remaining silent about the gold.

I have no choice. I am leaving town. I will disappear forever. I have the treasure of gold and I will slip away late in the night. I love you, Brad Webster. I am crushed and heartbroken to leave you....

One

Was he going to change history? Thomas Devlin reflected as he turned his red pickup off the Texas state highway.

On a brisk November day Tom drove through Windcroft's iron gates and followed a gravel road. As he looked around, a sense of wonder gripped him. A Devlin had not legally set foot on the Windcroft horse farm for a hundred years. During that time the families had engaged in a bitter feud, and now he was embroiled in it.

"You can still turn around and go home," he told himself aloud, his gaze traveling across Windcroft property that appeared so similar to Devlin land.

He looked at miles of mesquite-covered fields, the small trees bent because of prevailing southern winds. He liked the wide-open spaces and the blazing sunsets. He intended to settle here and had already bought a ranch that would soon be in his possession.

He liked the warmhearted people and his family. His uncle, Lucas Devlin, was levelheaded, friendly, a good man. Lucas worried that Tom's peace mission this morning was foolhardy, because his own overtures for conciliation with Will Windcroft had been rebuffed. Nothing tried, nothing gained, Tom thought.

Windcroft. Not a common name, but not uncommon either. It conjured up a Windcroft he had met five months ago at a Houston computer conference where he had been keynote speaker. A twenty-eight-year-old, violet-eyed, black-haired beauty with whom he had spent a wildly passionate night. To his surprise, he hadn't been able to forget her when it was usually easy for him to walk away. They had intended to exchange phone numbers, but he had been called away unexpectedly when one of his clients had vanished in the jungles of Colombia. Tom remembered that Rose Windcroft lived in Dallas. It might be like finding a needle in a haystack to locate her in the Dallas-Fort Worth area, but he intended to give it a try soon.

Erotic memories taunted him as he recalled too clearly the moment he had unzipped and slipped her silky black dress off her shoulders. Heat had consumed him when he'd looked at her full breasts pushed against the lacy bra she wore and the tiny strip of a thong that left most of her sensational body bare.

In his arms she had been wild, eager, and given him a red-hot night of sex that, too often since then, had made him wish he had her phone number.

When his pickup bounced over a bump in the road, he jerked his thoughts back to the approaching meeting with the West Texas Windcrofts. It probably wouldn't be an easy one.

Tom turned a bend and drove down a dip to cross a muddy creek. Beyond the creek, a shiny black car was parked off to the side, near the fencerow that paralleled the road.

A dozen horses were on the other side of the white PVC fencing, and one stood quietly while a woman petted it. Wondering if the woman was Nita Windcroft Thorne, who was supposed to be at the meeting, Tom glanced in that direction as his truck whipped by.

She twisted slightly to look over her shoulder, her chin-length black hair shiny in the sunlight. Snug jeans clung to her long legs and she wore a blue cotton shirt with a hip-length denim jacket.

He couldn't get his breath and his heart pounded. He knew her. Even from the distance he could see the violet-blue eyes—or did he just remember them? He slammed on the brakes, then wished he hadn't as gravel flew and dust stirred. When he backed up, she continued to watch him. Lucas had referred to Nita Windcroft a lot, but he had never mentioned Rose. Rose Windcroft, hot and sexy—and if she was standing here on Windcroft land, she had to be a member of the West Texas Windcrofts!

Tom parked in front of her car and climbed out, his pulse accelerating with each step he took. Rose Windcroft. It was *her*. The woman of one magic night and, afterward, his erotic dreams and fiery longings.

He knew the moment she recognized him. Her mouth opened, and he felt that his surprise was nothing compared to her reaction. Her face flushed, her jaw dropped farther and she blinked rapidly. Dimly in his mind he thought that she should never play poker because her expression gave away her thoughts as much as if she had voiced them.

"What are you doing here?" she asked breathlessly.

He was beginning to gather his wits and he smiled while his gaze swept over her one more time. "Looking at the sexiest woman in Texas and thinking this is my lucky day," he said in a husky voice. Her mere presence stirred physical responses in him.

She flushed a brighter pink, closed her mouth and became more composed. "That doesn't answer my question," she said coolly, and her manner puzzled him.

"You're a Windcroft," he said. "A Texas Windcroft."

"You knew that."

"From what you told me, you live and work in Dallas. I didn't know you're related to this particular family."

"I came home because my father and my sister are having some difficulties."

Wanting to be closer, Tom walked up to her. Her perfume beckoned him to come closer, and he had to fight the urge to wrap his arms around her.

"What are you doing here?" she blurted in a tone that she might use if she discovered a trespasser on the property.

"I have a meeting with your family concerning the feud," he replied patiently, certain she already knew why he was here.

"You're related to the Devlins." Turning pale, looking as upset and shocked as if he had struck her, she winced and stepped back. Her gaze ran over his features. "My God, you're a Devlin!" she repeated.

"You're right, I am a Devlin. Isn't that a surprise? I'm Lucas's nephew. When I was born, my mother gave me up for adoption. Frankly I'm damn glad to find this family," he said, his curiosity mounting, wondering if she was that much into the old feud. "You're surely not taken aback because of the feud. You can't consider me an enemy."

There was no mistaking when her eyes flashed with fire. "That's an understatement for how shocked I am," she said.

"At the time we met I didn't know my true background," he replied patiently, surprised that a generations-old feud stirred her emotions. Lucas could see the pointlessness in it—why couldn't Rose, especially when she didn't even live here? Frowning at him, she inhaled deeply, and he all but forgot their conversation as her breasts strained against the fabric of her shirt. His gaze went to her wide mouth and full, sensuous lips, and his temperature climbed. He could feel the electricity snap between them.

"Closed adoptions make it very difficult to locate parents," he continued. "Besides, I figured if someone gave me up at birth, they didn't want me to reappear and try to claim them years later." Open at the throat, her top revealed her creamy skin and cleavage, the beginning of the curves of her full breasts. When his hand touched her, her eyes darkened. He heard her quick intake of breath, and satisfaction as well as desire heated him.

"Lucas came searching for me." Tom lowered his voice. "Judging from the looks of it, you'd rather he hadn't found me."

"I'm surprised," she said, but there was hesitancy in her voice, and her glance slid away, causing him to wonder what she was hiding. She appeared to be choosing her words carefully and avoiding mentioning something to him, but he couldn't imagine what.

"No one has mentioned a Tom Morgan since I arrived. I've heard them speak of Tom Devlin." Her gaze bored into him.

"I thought I'd use the Devlin name. I have a blood family who wants to claim me and I'd like to claim them."

"Do you realize that a Devlin hasn't set foot on this land for almost a hundred years?"

"Then it's time one did. When we meet today, I want to talk to your father and sister, and hopefully you, about ending the feud."

"That's impossible! For months now Devlins have been playing havoc with the Windcrofts. That's why I've moved back."

His pulse jumped again. "You live here now?"

"Yes. I've come home to see about the trouble and help take care of my father. Daddy has a broken leg because of a Devlin," Rose snapped, and fires blazed in the depths of her eyes.

"We're not responsible for any of the calamities that have been happening to your family. My uncle and my cousins swear they're not involved, and I believe them. I promise you, we're not."

"I hope you mean what you say," she said softly.

"There," he said, lowering his voice. "Finally. That's the way I remember you. Our time together was the most fantastic evening in my life," he declared. Images of her naked in his arms danced in his inner vision. She had a fabulous body, and he ached to press her against him.

Again, her thickly lashed eyes darkened with pleasure. Her lips parted and she licked them. "It was special," she whispered.

"Go to dinner with me," he said.

She hesitated and frowned, puzzling him. He tilted his head, studying her. "Something's wrong. Have you met another man?" he asked, surprised how much her answer mattered to him.

She shook her head. "You're a Devlin even if you're called Tom Morgan."

"Surely you're not influenced by the feud that doesn't have anything to do with us. This is one Devlin who has no animosity toward the Windcrofts."

"Windcrofts and Devlins do not and have not associated with each other."

"So let's be the first to start patching things up," he argued with finality in his tone. He glanced at his watch. "I don't like to be late. We'll talk at the house. Are you staying here on the farm?"

There was an instant's hesitation before she nodded, and again he suspected something bothered her besides the family feud. "I live in the guesthouse," she said.

"That's where I'm staying on the Devlin ranch. If I don't leave now, I'm going to be late to see your father and sister." Even knowing it would delay him, he ached to kiss Rose. "Dammit. Come here, Rose," he said, slipping his arm around her waist, closing the distance. Her hands flew to his upper arms. When her eyelids fluttered and her lips parted, he knew she wanted the kiss as much as he did.

Excitement pulsed in him, a throbbing heat that gathered below his belt. He slipped his arm around her waist again and pressed her against him.

The moment his mouth touched hers, desire scalded him. He tightened his arm around her, bending over her and deepening his kiss, taking possession.

She wrapped her arms around his neck and wound her fingers in his hair. Her soft curves burned like a brand. He imagined her naked, loving with abandon. His tongue went deep, stroking her tongue. Aroused, he was rock-hard. He wanted her badly enough that he was tempted to make love to her right here and be damned the consequences.

She returned his kiss, her tongue going into his mouth, heightening his desire. She shook in his arms while her hips thrust against him and she moaned softly. Intense and hot, her responses sizzled. He slipped his hand beneath her jean jacket, sliding his fingers lightly over her breast and feeling the hardened bud pushing against the fabric. He twisted free the top buttons, slipping his hand beneath her blouse and cupping her breast.

She trembled and caught his wrist with one hand and pushed against his chest with the other.

He looked down at her. "If we weren't out here on the road and I didn't have an appointment with your family, I'd kiss away your objections," he declared. He trailed his lips to her ear. "I want to kiss every delicious inch of you."

She leaned back, and for a moment, such heat blazed in her eyes that he reached for her again. Shaking her head, she stepped away while she buttoned her blouse.

"You can't guess what you do to me," he said.

"You go now," she replied softly while her cheeks flushed a deeper pink.

His gaze lingered on her until he nodded and walked away. At his truck, he turned to look at her. With one hand on her hip and wind blowing locks of her black hair, she stood watching him. She took his breath away and he had to cool down before he met with anyone.

Tonight he would be with Rose. As he slid behind the wheel of his pickup, his eagerness to be with her surprised him. In the past he could walk away and forget a woman. He had always known there would soon be another appealing woman—the world was filled with them. But after meeting Rose, he hadn't been able to forget her and other women paled in comparison.

When he drove away, he glanced in the rearview mirror. She was already in her car and pulling onto the road behind him. She would attend this meeting—something that he hadn't dreamed would happen.

Soon the Windcroft house, main barn, stables, corrals, stallion pens and training pens came into Tom's view. The horse farm appeared peaceful, yet he knew it was fraught with danger. Too many bad things had been happening to the Windcrofts. To Tom's way of thinking, someone was hoping to drive the Windcrofts off their land.

Tom passed white fences and turned up the circle drive to the stone-facade house that held a welcoming front porch with rockers and pots of fall flowers. When he stepped out of his pickup, he leaned against it to wait for Rose. Staring at the long curving limbs of a nearby oak, Tom suspected the tree was as old as the anger between the two families. Uncle Lucas swore there was no one in the Devlin family fanning the fires of the feud, and Tom believed him.

The hundred-year-old Devlin-Windcroft feud had ignited over a poker game where Richard Windcroft lost half his land to a cheating Nick Devlin and then Windcroft supposedly murdered Devlin. At that time Jessamine Golden, Royal's most notorious outlaw, stole a treasure of gold and disappeared. When the mayor vanished, it was rumored she'd murdered him. Through the years legend indicated that the hidden treasure was on Windcroft land, and Tom knew his uncle thought that speculation was behind all of the Windcrofts' recent trouble. Tom looked over the green acres and wondered where the treasure was hidden. His gaze swung back to the porch. If Jessamine Golden's treasure really did exist and was hidden on the Windcroft place, it could be anywhere—even beneath the house or barn.

As Tom mulled local history, Rose drove up and parked. She hurried to join him with that sassy walk that accelerated his pulse.

"This has turned into a morning I never expected," he said.

"You won't get my daddy to agree to peace between the two families."

"We'll see. I intend to try to persuade him to."

As they crossed the porch, the door swung open. Tom looked at a woman who bore a resemblance to Rose Windcroft and he was certain he faced her sister, Nita. Her gaze was direct, her chin raised, and he suspected she was a no-nonsense person as capable of running the horse farm as he had heard she was.

"Nita, this is Tom Devlin," Rose said. "Tom, meet my sister, Nita Thorne."

When Nita thrust out her hand, her eyebrows arched in surprise and she looked back and forth between Rose and him.

"How do you do," he said, shaking her hand. As he had expected, Nita's grip was firm.

"Do you two know each other?" Nita asked, looking at Rose, who nodded.

"Yes, we do. We met at a business convention a few months back," Rose replied in a casual tone. She turned to Tom. "Come in and meet Daddy."

Curious about where Rose had grown up, Tom entered a house that was contemporary and inviting. The grand foyer held an iron baluster split stairway that indicated Rose's past had a degree of luxury. Through extra-wide windows that ran almost to the ceiling, sunlight spilled into the spacious living room. A stone fireplace stood at one end of the room and adjacent to it sat a man with his leg in a cast, his foot propped on an ottoman.

Rose took Tom's arm. "Daddy, this is Tom Devlin, Lucas Devlin's nephew. Tom, meet Will Windcroft."

"You're damned lucky I have this broken leg or I'd run you out of here before you could say a word," Will groused.

"I'm here on a peace mission," Tom said politely, gazing at the man whose leathery appearance was a testament to how many hours he spent working out of doors. Beneath salt-and-pepper hair Will's eyes flashed with anger. Tom suspected he might have had to fend off a fist in his face if Will hadn't had a broken leg. "At least hear me out. In town they say you're a reasonable man. That's part of why I made this appointment. My family would like to end the feud."

"Like hell, they would!" Will snapped. "They're doing everything they can to promote it. Who else would tear down our fences and poison our feed and dig holes so my horse went down and took me with him? Get out of my house. I didn't agree to this meeting," he added with a glare toward Nita.

"Daddy," Nita said. "If Connor were here, he would urge you to listen."

"Wait a minute, Daddy," Rose insisted.

"It's not us doing bad and dangerous things to Windcrofts," Tom continued calmly. "Give me half an hour to talk, Mr. Windcroft. I have information that might change your mind."

Will said a blunt and crude word.

"I think we ought to listen," Nita urged. "Connor believes Tom."

"That's because they're both in the Cattleman's Club. And you believe Connor because you just married him. I'm not listening to a bunch of bull, and you can get out of our house!" Will's voice rose, his face flushing.

"Sir," Tom said firmly, "if you don't hear me out, you have a lot to lose. Your mishap could've had worse consequences. Next time, if something terrible happens to Rose or Nita and you learn the Devlins aren't responsible, you'll hate yourself for not doing what you could've to prevent a tragedy. If you listen, you have everything to gain."

In silence Will scowled at Tom.

"I think you know that we've had one murder—Jonathan Devlin," Tom continued in a quiet, assertive voice. "Uncle Lucas doesn't think it was a Windcroft who killed his grandfather. This may not be a Devlin-Windcroft battle after all."

Will sighed. "All right. Sit down and let's hear what you have to say."

Two

"Thanks, Mr. Windcroft," Tom replied, glancing at Rose.

When Tom looked into her eyes, Rose Windcroft's pulse jumped. Unable to tear her gaze away, she watched him cross the room. Tall, commanding, with sexy, melt-your-bones gray eyes, he made her pulse leap as much now as that first moment they had met at the Houston computer convention. This time he was casually dressed in a leather bomber jacket, a long-sleeved red-and-navy-plaid shirt and jeans.

Tom offered his hand to her father, who glared at him without shaking hands. "Tell me what you came to tell me," Will said bluntly.

Tom was a Devlin! Rose was still stunned. One shock right after another. Her problems had compounded a thousandfold. She brushed her hand across her stomach.

How could she have brought such upheaval into her life? The answer was crossing her living room—a virile, handsome, irresistible male who had made passionate love to her and gotten her pregnant!

Tom had used condoms, but Dr. Amos Hartley had carefully explained to her that sometimes they broke or weren't handled properly—a fact she already knew but hadn't thought would ever apply to her.

She hadn't informed her family of her condition, and here was Tom Morgan in her life again and living on a nearby ranch. And not Tom Morgan, but Tom Devlin.

She had decided earlier today that she would announce her pregnancy to her family. There was no use in delaying any longer. She now had to think about telling Tom soon too. She dreaded revealing the truth to Tom because the last thing she wanted was a man to offer marriage out of a sense of duty.

She recalled how she and Tom had intended to exchange phone numbers, but she had had to leave the conference early because of a lucrative contract she was getting. The client had called and agreed to go with Rose's company, and Rose had to be present to sign the deal. With all that had happened since then, the conference seemed longer ago than five months.

Drinking in the sight of Tom, she inhaled while a pang of longing tore at her. When he had approached her at the side of the road, how she had wanted to throw herself into his arms.

"I'm sorry about all that's happened," Tom said as he sat in a chair facing Will.

On edge, Rose doubted her father would listen to Tom. Will sat with his lips clamped together, his chin raised as Rose had seen him do too many times before. She knew the gesture meant not only *no* but also *hell, no!*

While the men talked, she thought about Tom asking her to dinner—anticipation made her heart race, yet she knew she shouldn't go out with him again. Truce or not, it was difficult to spend time with a Devlin because she had grown up hating them. As she gazed at Tom, she received a look in return that sent a current charging down to her toes. She tried to concentrate on what he was saying to her father.

"We didn't do any of the things that have been happening here lately, and both families need to find out who's behind the incidents and why," Tom said. "We can join forces to catch the culprit."

"I don't know what you have to gain by this, but I'm not falling for some line of lies from a Devlin," Will snapped.

"Sir, my uncle Lucas was going through Jonathan's things and found some odd notations in the book so the entries were vague but mentioned payments Jonathan had been receiving from an unknown source. Lucas also found letters to Jonathan, and I brought one with me for you to see."

Tom got up, pulled paper from a jacket pocket and handed Will the wrinkled letter. As Tom bent down to draw his finger along a line of writing, Rose went to stand behind her father and read over his shoulder. Nita pulled her chair close to read also.

"See, it mentions a payment," Tom said. "Then look at the next paragraph."

Rose read aloud, "There could be trouble if the Windcrofts ever find the diary or know the truth." Rose looked up at Tom. "A diary?"

"No one has discovered a diary. Read farther down the page," Tom instructed.

She leaned over her father's shoulder again and continued, "The only way to survive is to keep the feud going between the Windcrofts and the Devlins. That is imperative."

Surprised, Rose gave Tom another startled look.

"That's all," Tom said. "There's nothing else to indicate the Devlins aren't involved, but that, plus my uncle's word, should be enough to convince you peace between us is worth a try. Let's declare an armistice and together, see if we can catch whoever is behind the disasters here," Tom added, looking into Rose's eyes before he returned to his chair.

"That's not much, but it's something," Will grudgingly agreed, reading the letter again. Rose had never before considered the possibility that the Devlins were telling the truth. Suppose they weren't guilty, and it was someone else who wanted to hurt Nita and her father?

Will's expression was solemn. "What would anyone have to gain by fanning the feud?"

"That's one of the questions we need answered," Tom said. "Someone may want to run you folks off this land."

"Why?" Rose asked, and Will and Nita exchanged a look.

"That old legend about Jessamine Golden's hidden treasure," Nita replied.

"All the current trouble surfaced at the time of Royal's one hundred and twenty-fifth. anniversary," Will explained. "Six months before the anniversary Jonathan Devlin died. Later, items were found in a trunk in his attic. They were historical artifacts that had belonged to Jessamine Golden."

"When the artifacts were found, rumors started flying," Nita added. "An anniversary ball and fund-raiser had been scheduled. The artifacts were donated for the charity auction and since have been given to the Historical Society Museum, but there's still talk about hidden gold."

"I figured that's legend and nothing more," Rose said and was surprised when Will shook his head.

"A lot of people give credence to the stories. Among Jessamine's things there is a map that indicates the existence of the treasure. I've seen a copy of the map and I recognized our land," Will explained.

"Whether the gold exists or not," Tom said, "someone is willing to kill to find it."

"Jessamine's map doesn't reveal where the gold is hidden. Something is missing," Will said. "There must be something that goes with the map that shows the location."

Wondering how much danger all of them were in, Rose rubbed her arms. She was frightened for her father and sister, who had roamed the horse farm by themselves almost daily until her daddy had broken his leg.

Will frowned and picked up the letter to read it again, while Rose moved to a wing chair. One look at Nita, and Rose knew that they were in agreement with Tom. Otherwise, Nita's chin would be thrust out and fire would be in her eyes.

"I think we should consider a truce," Rose said, although part of her wondered if they were being taken in by a smooth-talking Devlin.

"If we call off the feud, we won't stop guarding the farm or anything like that," Nita remarked.

"I don't think you should. It's obvious someone is trying to harm you folks and cause you trouble. You may be in a lot of danger," Tom replied, looking at Rose. "But if our two families cooperate, there will be more of us to hear rumors or watch for anything amiss. Lucas said he can spare some of our men to patrol your grounds."

"Daddy, that would be a help," Rose said solemnly.

Will nodded his head. "All right. Temporarily maybe, but we'll accept Devlin help and friendship."

How many surprises would this day hold? Rose wondered. The Devlins and the Windcrofts working together! She glanced at Tom and found him watching her with an intentness that curled her toes.

"Thanks, Mr. Windcroft," he said, shifting his attention to her father. "I don't think you'll regret your decision. I'll tell Lucas. Any leads anyone has, we'll pool our information. Connor and I will stay in contact."

"I hope you're leveling with me," Will said flatly. "If you're not…" The unspoken threat hung in the air.

"I am, sir," Tom replied. "I promise you—I'm not a part of any feud with the Windcrofts and never have been. I didn't know I was a Devlin until a few months ago, and there are no reasons for me to hate a member of your family," he added quietly. "If you can think of any enemies you might have, it would be helpful."

"We've tried and we've given the sheriff and Connor even the remotest possibilities," Nita stated.

Nodding, Tom stood. "I'll go now. It was nice to finally meet you," he said, offering his hand to Will.

When he reached out to shake Tom's hand, Rose let out her breath. In the quiet of their living room, a historic moment that might change their lives forever had taken place—after a century, there was no Windcroft-Devlin feud.

Tom told Nita that he was glad to have met her and then he looked at Rose.

"Rose and I already know each other," he said. Her father turned to stare at her.

"We met at a recent business convention in Houston," Rose explained.

"You're another computer person," Nita remarked.

"Actually not," Rose answered before Tom could. "Tom was the keynote speaker. He's in demolition, not computers." She headed out of the room. "I'll go to the door with you," she said, knowing she would return to questions from her father and Nita, although Nita was so much in love with Connor, she didn't pay much attention to people and things around her.

Rose and Tom walked down the hall to the front door and out onto the porch. She studied his thick black hair and his unusual smoky-gray eyes. She should have known he was a Devlin—he bore a resemblance to them. He was better-looking, taller and had a squarer jaw. Her mind spun with the knowledge of who he was, and memories of the most exciting man she had ever known tormented her.

She turned to Tom. "Well, you got what you wanted."

"Thank God. I think your family is in danger, and the incidents are getting more disastrous. Your father could've been hurt worse than he was when his horse fell in that hole. The same was true when Nita's brake line was cut."

"That's why I'm home—to help and support wherever I can," Rose replied solemnly. "I've moved my business here and have my computers set up in the guesthouse. This is the advantage of having your own business. As you well know, if you hire the right people, they can run things when you're away."

"How many people work for you?"

"Five. We have a small Dallas office where we do computer programming and also some graphic work."

"You can tell me more about it tonight. I'll pick you up around seven."

Half of her yearned to give him a big smile and agree while the other half of her screamed warnings not to go. She started to say no, but before she could, he kissed her, covering her mouth with his. The moment their lips touched, her heart thudded. She longed to wrap her arms around him and kiss him in return.

She wanted to announce that she was carrying their baby—the one they'd made together that night—but she wasn't quite ready to face the emotional upheaval her announcement would bring. She had to face the grim fact that he eventually would learn the truth. It wouldn't be long until she couldn't hide her pregnancy at all.

Then all thought fled, demolished by his kiss. His strong fingers wound in her hair while his arm banded her tightly. Suddenly he stopped. His gaze was intense, hungry for love. She could see that he wanted her. "I'll be here at seven," he said gruffly.

While he waited, silence stretched, and once again she knew she had the opportunity to refuse right now, to end this. Yet the words wouldn't come. Tom's satisfaction was evident in his expression when he gave her a faint smile, then moved away.

In long strides he walked to his pickup, and as she watched him climb in then drive away, she remembered that Houston encounter as if it had just happened. They both had been headed to the hotel's indoor swimming pool. She had stepped out of the elevator at the same time he appeared around a corner.

When they collided, his hands went out to steady her. Transfixed, she looked into thickly lashed eyes the color of smoke from a wood fire. She was conscious of his hands on her arms, his bare chest only inches from her. When his gaze lowered to her unfastened swimsuit cover-up, he inhaled deeply.

"I hope you're not hurt," he said, and she shook her head, "because I'm glad I ran into you. I would've been to the pool sooner if I'd known you were here." His voice was deep as he spoke in a lazy drawl. His gaze strayed to her mouth, then drifted down over her, and she couldn't get her breath.

"That's the best-looking cover-up I've ever seen," he said softly.

"Thank you," she replied, while her temperature rose another notch because she knew he wasn't referring to her cover-up but to her. He was a sexy male with sculpted muscles and rugged good looks.

"I'm Tom Morgan."

"I'm Rose Windcroft."

"So we're going to swim together." His voice became more throaty with an innuendo that implied they were going to do something together more intimate than swimming.

This handsome Tom Morgan was flirting with her, and an uncustomary recklessness made her receptive to him.

"I can't wait to get together...to swim," she added in a breathless whisper, toying with him in return. When she did, something dark shifted in the depths of his eyes, and his heated look set her pulse pounding.

"Where are you from?" he asked.

"I live in Dallas." Barely able to get out the words,

she knew she was taunting a tiger and she should stop before she was devoured.

"I'm in Dallas occasionally on business. I can be there when it's not business. I'll have to visit Dallas soon so we can—" he paused, and her heart thudded while possibilities for what she would like to do with him ran through her thoughts "—swim together again," he finished.

"Speaking of swimming—that's what I came here to do," she said, walking past him. He caught up to her and reached around to open the glass door for her.

"We can't get in," Tom said in surprise.

They both peered through the glass walls into the deserted room with its large, sparkling blue tiled pool, but no one was inside. Tom glanced at the posted sign on the wall.

"According to the schedule, this room should be open," he said. "I'll go ask at the desk."

In seconds he was back. Walking beside him was a man in a yellow jumpsuit emblazoned with the hotel logo. "Sorry about that," the hotel employee said. "We closed to clean the pool and someone forgot to open the room again."

They both thanked him and entered the pool area. She dropped her towel, shed her cover-up, then turned to find Tom openly watching her, his appreciative gaze moving leisurely over her brief swimsuit.

She was just as ensnared by his terrific, muscled body. His biceps bulged, and his chest was well-defined with a smattering of short black hair. He was fit, and the tiny swimming trunks barely covered his well-endowed masculinity.

"Race you to the end of the pool," he said. "I'll give you a head start."

"I don't need a head start," she flung back at him, then sliced into the water and swam as swiftly as she could, wanting to win the race, feeling a competitive excitement.

Out of the corner of her eye she saw him pass her, then pull ahead. When they reached the end, he caught her, holding her up while he treaded water. His hands were on her waist, his thumbs below her breasts, close enough to tantalize, and her desire blazed.

"Let me take you to dinner tonight," he suggested.

"I barely know you."

"We'll eat here at the hotel, and I'll introduce you to people who do know me. I'm the keynote speaker in the morning."

She knew the keynote was not from the computer industry, but she couldn't recall what his vocation was. *"Sorry, I didn't recognize your name."*

He smiled, revealing even white teeth, while appealing creases bracketed his mouth. *"You shouldn't be expected to recognize it. We're not in the same business. I'm a demolition contractor."*

"You tear things down."

"Not everything, only what I'm hired to demolish. But then, there's another kind of destruction," he said in a deeper voice and pulled her closer. Her legs tangled with his and she put her hands on his upper arms, feeling his warm, wet skin. *"The kind I'd like to do to you and the kind I know you can do to me,"* he said in a thick voice, his gaze lowering again to her mouth.

With a pounding heart she wriggled and swam away, smiling at him. *"You're flirting,"* she stated breathlessly, trying to curb the devastating effect he was having on her.

He smiled in return and swam toward her. *"Go to dinner with me."*

"Since I know who you are and I've heard people at work discuss you, I will."

"Seven o'clock." He paused before confessing, "I have to say, this conference suddenly has gotten a whole lot better."

"I agree," she said, then turned to swim the length of the pool.

For another thirty minutes they swam, then climbed out to get dressed for their dinner together.

"I'll meet you in the lobby at seven," she said when they were in the elevator, trying to keep from letting her gaze roam over his muscled chest again and down even lower.

"I can come to your room," he said, looking at her with the thorough study that she was trying to avoid giving him.

"In the lobby," she replied firmly and left the elevator with her pulse racing. An hour later when she entered the lobby, he was already there. Wearing a navy suit and snowy white shirt, he was handsome and commanding.

What an evening she'd had with him. The moment she had walked into his arms for their first dance, she had been electrified. Sparks spun in the air, and she knew he felt the fiery contact, too.

Now, desire was a scalding flame again. She hadn't been able to resist him the first night, wondering who seduced whom. He was a fantastic lover with a body that could win him a movie role.

"You must know him pretty well," a raspy feminine voice spoke behind Rose.

"I suppose." She turned to look at her younger sister. Because of the age gap between them and the difference in their personalities, they hadn't been particularly close growing up. Nita was the tomboy and horse expert while Rose was the people person and the one who had longed for city life. Nita was Daddy's girl and Rose never had been. She had finally matured enough to acknowledge her jealousy of the close relationship between Nita and their father.

"What do you think?" Nita asked. "You obviously believe him."

"I didn't know he was a Devlin until this morning," Rose answered, taking a deep breath and knowing she had put this moment off long enough. Nita began to pull a few wilted leaves off yellow chrysanthemums growing in a nearby pot.

"Nita, this danger to you and Daddy and the farm isn't my only worry."

"Oh? This sounds serious," Nita said as she tossed the dead leaves off the porch, then leaned against a cedar column.

"Even before I came home, I tried to figure out the best way to tell you and Daddy something special. I need to tell Jane, too," Rose said, thinking about their former housekeeper who was now married to Will.

"I'm getting more curious. Rose, you know you can tell me anything. Are you unwell? Are you moving away from Texas?"

"I'm not moving and I feel fine most of the time."

Worry clouded Nita's eyes. "*Most* of the time? What is it? Can I do something to help?"

"Thanks. You can't do anything. Unfortunately I got myself into this one," Rose replied, taking another deep breath. "There isn't a good way to say this except to come right out with it. Nita, I'm pregnant."

Nita shrieked and threw her arms around Rose. When she leaned back to look at her sister, Nita's eyes sparkled. "That's wonderful! You've been keeping a lot from us. Who's the lucky guy?"

"There isn't any 'lucky guy' because I didn't intend for this to happen," Rose replied, hating to reveal the truth.

Nita's smile vanished, and she stepped back to stare wide-eyed at her sister. "Oh, Rose! You're usually so in control."

"Well, I should have been more in control this time."

"What's he said? He doesn't want to get married?"

"He doesn't know. Nita, would you want a guy to marry you out of a sense of obligation? As independent as you are, you know you wouldn't want someone to propose to you because he felt beholden to do so. We're not in love. Actually I hardly know him."

"Oh, Rose!" Nita exclaimed again. "Damn, I'm sorry. Maybe you should rethink not telling him."

"I know I'll have to eventually, but this isn't turning out the way I've always dreamed it would. I intended to wait to get married until I was at least thirty, probably thirty-five. I still want my freedom and I'm not ready for marriage. Besides, I want to make the important life decisions for this baby and I don't know this man well enough to predict how he'll act or what he'll want. I'm not about to compromise on what I think is best for the baby."

"If you feel that way, you know you may end up being lonely and find life difficult. You should at least think about your options before you lock up your heart. Marriage isn't about losing control. Look at me. I'm so in love with Connor—marriage is wonderful."

"And that's the way I want my marriage to be—two people wildly in love," Rose argued, still hurting over her shattered dreams. "I want a love match—not a couple who weds because they feel obligated. The statistics are scary enough when one out of two marriages ends in divorce. The statistics are higher if the marriage occurs because of a child."

"I think you're looking at the worst-case scenarios," Nita said.

"Right now, marriage is absolutely out of the question for all those reasons. But most of all because it means losing my control to someone I don't know well enough. I told you—no, thanks."

"Whatever you choose to do, we love you and we'll love your baby. You know that," Nita said, and Rose had never felt such a strong bond with her sister.

"Thank you. I knew I could count on you to support me in this," Rose said and realized that, in spite of sibling rivalries, she could always bank on Nita when a crisis threatened.

"Of course I'll support you," Nita exclaimed. "So will Daddy and Jane." She placed her hands on her hips. "How far along are you?"

"Five months," Rose replied.

"Five! You don't look pregnant at all."

"My waist is starting to get bigger—only a little." She patted her middle. "The father has a right to know and eventually I'll inform him, but at the moment I'm getting used to all this myself."

"Do you know what you're having?"

"A girl," Rose said and smiled. "More females in this family."

"That's wonderful!"

Rose frowned. "Nita, I don't want to tell Daddy. Jane will be easier, but Daddy is going to be unhappy. This isn't what he'd want for me."

"You have to tell him."

"I dread it. You know Daddy. He'll want to go after the man responsible with a shotgun. And he's distressed already. I know the farm can't take many more disasters. It has to be hurting financially. It is, isn't it?"

Nita inhaled deeply and looked beyond Rose before her gaze swung back to her sister. "It was, but Connor keeps telling me to stop stewing over income. He's invested in the horse farm to bring it back up to speed, so now he's part owner and we have his financial backing."

"Thank goodness! That's one concern off my mind."

"I don't want Daddy to fret either and I don't want him to try to do something he shouldn't or, worse, try to get around on his leg too soon," Nita said. "A baby is different from worrying about the farm's finances or the catastrophes that have been happening. After the first shock, he'll be happy. You know he's going to adore a grandchild."

"I don't know that."

"He will, and I think you should tell him now."

Rose gazed down the drive, remembering watching Tom leave. She knew what she had to do and it *had* been a relief to tell Nita her secret. "I guess I will. It's not going to get any easier."

"What's not going to get any easier?" Will asked as he hobbled onto the porch, swinging his crutches with each step. "I thought I'd sit out here. I get tired of being cooped up in the house, but maybe I'm interrupting something," he said. "I can come back later."

"Not at all," Rose said. She took a deep breath and balled her fists.

"Come sit down. I have something to tell you."

Three

"Sure." He crossed to a chaise longue and as he scooted into it, Nita helped him prop up his leg. When he looked at Rose expectantly, she wished with all her being she didn't have to tell him her secret. As the silence stretched, Will arched his eyebrows.

"Rose, Daddy and I love you," Nita said softly, stepping close to her sister and putting her arm around Rose's shoulders. Will frowned and looked from one daughter to the other.

"Now you've got me worried," he said. "Of course we love you. What is it, honey?"

"There's no easy way to tell you."

"Well, then, go ahead and say whatever is worrying you."

"I'm pregnant," she blurted out the announcement, holding her breath and afraid he would be unhappy to hear her news.

His eyes widened. "That's great, Rose!" He struggled to his feet again, awkwardly trying to hug her and hang on to one of his crutches at the same time. "That's wonderful!" He held her away to look at her and tilted his head, studying her. As his smile faded, he picked up her hand. "I don't see a wedding ring."

"No, you don't."

"You're not getting married, are you?" he asked in a quiet voice.

She shook her head. "No, I'm not." She hurt when he winced, yet at the same time a weight had been lifted from her by finally informing her family about her condition.

"Rose, that's going to be so damned hard for you. Being a single parent is tough. I should know. Dammit, he ought to marry you," Will said, anger filling his voice. His eyes darkened, and she could see an emotional storm coming.

"It's my choice," she said. "He doesn't even know I'm pregnant."

"Tell him, for Lord's sake. By damn—"

"Daddy, I don't want to marry him," Rose said firmly, but her father's remark about being a single parent struck a chill in her heart. She hated failure and had spent her life trying to prove herself—maybe to her father because he had been so easily pleased by Nita, who was practically the son he'd always wanted as well as a daughter to him.

Rose pushed her trepidation aside, telling herself she had excelled at other endeavors, she could succeed as a single parent. She had bought over a dozen books on motherhood and was studying about pregnancy, babies and becoming a parent.

"Let's sit down, Daddy," Nita urged, taking her father's arm to help him back to the chaise and prop his foot up again. He motioned to another chair.

"You two sit down and we'll make some plans. You'll stay here to have the baby, won't you?"

"I haven't planned that far ahead—I'm only five months along. I don't know what I'm going to do," Rose answered.

"You're going to stay home and have this baby here, where we can all help and support you."

"I agree with Daddy," Nita said firmly. In that moment Rose appreciated her younger sister more than she ever had before.

"You two!" Rose exclaimed. "I'll be all right."

"Damn straight you will, because we'll take care of you," Nita declared, and Rose had to smile.

"I'm fine. The morning sickness is beginning to fade away and other than that, I'm okay. There is one thing—"

"What's that?" Will asked her. "Don't hesitate to ask."

"I don't want to inform other people yet. I'm getting used to the idea myself and I've been spending all my time trying to think how to tell all of you. Of course, Connor can know, but I'd like to keep the knowledge here on the farm for now."

"We can do that," Nita said.

"We sure as hell can." Will seconded her. "Whatever you want, you let us know."

"That means so much to me, coming from both of you," Rose said.

"Rose, tell Daddy what you're having," Nita said, glancing at Will.

"My baby is a girl."

"A granddaughter! Ah, Rose, that's grand. A little

girl," Will said and had such tenderness in his voice that Rose relaxed and tears stung her eyes.

"I have to tell Jane," she said, knowing because of the closeness to Jane, dealing with her would be easier.

"Jane will be overjoyed," Will said and Nita agreed.

"She'll want to take care of you, too."

"I don't know. Jane can be kind of fierce sometimes."

"That's when someone interferes with her or her afternoon reading time. She's going to love a baby girl," Nita said.

"You're five months," Will said. "So the baby is due early next spring." He slapped his knee and grinned. "I'm going to be a granddaddy! It'll be good, Rose, because there are a lot of us to love her."

"Thank you both," Rose said, relieved and grateful for their reassurances.

"I'm sure you know your own mind, but have you given a lot of thought to the father?" Will asked. "Are you absolutely certain you're not in love with him?"

"I'm sure I'm not," she said, wanting to escape telling her father that there would be Devlin blood in the Windcroft family. She had hoped to avoid revealing the father's identity, and now, with Tom on a nearby ranch, she knew she would see him occasionally. Remembering that she shouldn't look anxious or unhappy in front of her family, Rose smiled.

"Who's your doctor?" Will asked.

"It's Amos Hartley in Dallas. I like him very much."

"You can't live here and have a doctor in Dallas," Will stated. "We'll find an excellent one in Royal. Nita, I'll leave that to you because you're in the right age group to hear baby doctors discussed. All I know are vets," he added with a grin.

"I can find a doctor for myself," Rose said with amusement. She was aware her father and sister both watched her intently. "And I feel fine. I'm all right. Truly." She stood. "Since I'm going out tonight with Tom, I better go get ready." She went to brush a kiss on her father's forehead. He caught her hand in his and squeezed lightly.

"I want you to be happy. You consider the father, Rose."

"Don't get false hopes," she said. "He wouldn't want to marry me, and I don't want to marry him," she said emphatically, trying to end any conversation on the subject.

"Okay," Will said solemnly and the distress had returned to his expression. "We'll abide by your wishes and not tell others until you're ready."

"We'll all help you," Nita said.

Rose turned to hug Nita. "Thanks, Nita. Your support means the world."

"Can I bring you anything, Rose? Is there anything you need?" Nita asked, and Rose had to laugh at the earnest expression on her sister's face.

"I'm fine. Don't fuss over me."

"I wonder if you ought to move up here in the house with us," Will said.

"No, I don't need to leave the guesthouse," she replied patiently. "I'm not an invalid and I have my computer and electronic equipment all set up where I am." She didn't add that they were all newlyweds and she thought she ought to leave them as much privacy as possible. "I'm going to find Jane now."

Following some delicious smells, she headed to the kitchen. Rose was certain she had left Nita and their father making all sorts of plans about her pregnancy and the baby. But would those plans continue with the same enthusiasm once her daddy learned who had fathered his grandchild? Will's fuse likely would light and he would try to involve Tom in Rose's life one way or another. She shuddered because that was the last thing she wanted.

When she entered the kitchen, she saw Jane close the oven door and go to the refrigerator to remove a head of lettuce.

"Jane, can I talk to you a moment?" Rose asked.

"Sure, honey," Jane replied, flashing a smile at Rose and going back to work. "I'm still astounded by the latest turn of events. Your daddy told me that he agreed to peace between the families. I never thought I'd see the day. Tom Devlin must be some persuasive talker. This morning your Daddy was so dead set against even listening to a Devlin, I didn't think anyone could convince him otherwise." She shook her head. "Wonders never cease. But maybe it's for the best."

"If it isn't Devlins doing all the bad things to us," Rose said, "then this may give us a better chance to catch who is behind the trouble. And the Devlins will help us guard the horse farm."

"I hope we nab the rascals and they rot in jail. Or worse," Jane said darkly. Rose knew while Jane's loyalties to those she loved could be unbreakable, her anger with those she didn't like could be ferocious.

"You're in for another surprise today," Rose said quietly.

Jane's eyebrows arched as she dried her hands and turned to study Rose. "This sounds like big news," she said.

"It is." Rose took a deep breath. "I'm pregnant."

Jane's eyes opened wider. She recovered her surprise and grinned, walking over to hug Rose. "That's wonderful! Will is going to bust his buttons with joy!"

She squinted her eyes, studying Rose once more. "You're not marrying the father, are you?"

Rose shook her head. "No. We're not in love. We barely know each other. I don't want to marry a man because he feels a sense of obligation. That would be dreadful. I always expected to be deeply in love when I married."

"Rose, don't deny your baby a father if there's any possibility of working things out," Jane said solemnly.

"I won't. I'm certain about this."

"I know you, Rose. You don't want to share the decision-making concerning this baby. You want to control the situation yourself."

Rose sighed. "Leave it to you to recognize that."

"Honey, you're going to find that babies have a way of demolishing adults' plans and preconceived notions. Let go a little." Suddenly Jane grinned and hugged Rose again. "I know your daddy will pop with joy. Nita, too." Jane stepped back to look at Rose. "How far along are you? Two or three months?"

"No, I'm five months."

"Lordy, you don't show."

"You look closely, you can tell, but I'm not very big yet. I've had an ultrasound."

"And? Boy or girl?"

"We're going to have another girl in the family," she announced, excitement bubbling in her now that her family knew. Their enthusiasm was infectious and added to her relief over their reactions.

"It'll be like having you and Nita all over again. Your daddy is going to be thrilled to have a granddaughter. If you need me for anything at all, you let me know. And tell me if you don't feel well. Do you hear?"

"Thanks, Jane. All of you don't have to fuss over me."

"We're going to fuss, so accept it."

Rose smiled and headed toward the door. "Don't worry about me for dinner. I'm going out with Tom Devlin tonight."

"Oh, my! A Devlin and a Windcroft. That will stir up a storm in town."

"Indeed, it will." Rose paused. "Jane, I'd prefer to keep news of my pregnancy in the family for a little while longer."

"Sure, Rose. Nita, Connor and I can do that, but how you will keep your Daddy from informing everyone he knows?"

"He promised to wait. It's been difficult enough to tell all of you. I need more time to prepare to disclose it to other people."

"Sure. Rose, we all love you and we'll love this baby until it's spoiled rotten," Jane said tenderly, and Rose nodded.

"Thanks, Jane. I know I can count on my family," she said and left, realizing that family was becoming more important to her by the day.

She turned toward the guesthouse, one set of worries changing swiftly to another set as she contemplated her evening.

Why had she agreed to go to dinner with Tom? She knew why. Not only did her racing pulse give her an answer, but for the same reason her father had agreed to an armistice—Tom Morgan-Devlin was devilishly persuasive.

What would it hurt if they saw each other?

It could damage plenty, she knew, by complicating her life if he found out that she was carrying his child

before she was ready to tell him. She knew she was putting off the inevitable, but she couldn't deal with him
yet. He was a forceful, aggressive, controlling male.
She had always dreamed of someday falling in love
with a man who was easygoing, settling in Dallas or
some large Texas city where she would be close to her
family but still live in an urban area. Tom didn't fit that
dream at all.

She didn't know him well enough to know how he
would react, but a hundred times a day the decision that
she didn't want to marry someone because he felt duty
bound to wed ran through her mind. She could manage
as a single parent. Her father had done it for years and
done a good job at it. Yet she had to admit that Jane had
been there to help him.

Rose let herself through the side gate to the guesthouse and crossed the wraparound porch to enter
through the large, high-ceilinged kitchen. She strode to
her bedroom, her thoughts completely on Tom as she
dressed for the evening.

When it was almost seven, Rose studied herself in the
mirror, turning first one way, then another before she
smiled in satisfaction. Her black hair was cut chin
length, curling toward her face and the black dress she
wore didn't cover her knees. Her stomach was beginning to be slightly rounded, but it wasn't obvious in her
loose-fitting dress. She had changed very little, except
that her skirts were tighter at the waist than before. But
hopefully Tom wasn't going to guess her condition. No
one else had.

She heard a car approach, then stop outside. A door
slammed and in seconds her doorbell rang. While her
heart jumped with excitement, she glanced once more

at her image. "You shouldn't be doing this," she whispered to her reflection, shaking her head, knowing that spending the evening with Tom was tempting fate and could bring a heap of trouble down on her. Until she told him the truth, she should avoid him like the plague. This was the last man on earth with whom she should be spending the evening.

Her racing heartbeat said otherwise.

She hurried to the front door. As she swung it open, she was dazzled by the sight of him. Wearing a charcoal suit, with his black hair neatly combed, he sent her pulse galloping even faster.

"Am I glad I came to West Texas," he said while his warm gaze drifted over her.

"Come in and I'll get my purse," she invited, stepping back.

"Sure," he replied, following her into a large knotty-pine-paneled family room, where she picked up her purse and turned to find him watching her intently.

"You look beautiful," he said softly.

"Thank you. And you look handsome," she added.

Crossing the room, he dominated the space around him and as he approached her, her heart thudded.

"Rose, I've missed you," he said, stopping close in front of her. His fingers closed around her upper arm and he drew her to him.

"Tom—"

"We can go to dinner in a little while. Let's finish what we started this afternoon," he said, his heated gaze boring into her. As he leaned toward her, Rose placed her hands against his chest.

"This morning we were impetuous," she said softly.

"We were spectacular together," he said. His gray

eyes held flames of desire. A little warning that she was getting more embroiled with him by the minute went off inside her. She really should be doing the opposite.

She shouldn't even be going to dinner with him. She didn't want him to learn about her pregnancy yet.

And the only way to avoid having him discover that she was pregnant was to stay far away from him. Too late now.

"Let's go to dinner," she insisted, but her voice was breathless. Without waiting to see if he was following, she turned to leave the room.

When he caught up with her, she saw amusement in his expression, but there was no mistaking the longing that burned in his eyes and made her heart pound.

"Nice house." he said.

"This was the first ranch house. Although rooms were added through the years. My mom never liked living out here on the farm, so Daddy built the new house for her."

"My uncle's house is like this one. It's the original structure that has been added to. I like staying on the ranch, but it's temporary."

"Do you have a job you have to go back to?"

One corner of Tom's mouth lifted in a lopsided grin. "Sure, but if I'm not there, I have employees who can run things efficiently. I just meant I can't live on the Devlin ranch permanently. I'd feel as if I were imposing on my uncle's hospitality. I have a condo in town and I've bought a ranch."

Startled, she missed a step and he steadied her as she looked up at him. "You're moving here permanently?"

"Yes, I am. I have to build a house on the land I've purchased, so I can't move there yet, but I'm staying in this part of the country. I love West Texas and everything about it. I want to be a rancher. I haven't decided yet if I'll sell my demolition business or just let others run it."

Shaken by the fact that he might be their neighbor soon, she was silent. While she wondered how knowledge about the baby would affect his decision to move, Rose locked up and they left the house. They climbed into a black sports car, and she settled in while Tom drove to Royal.

He had made reservations at Claire's, Royal's elegant French restaurant on Main. As they were seated at their table, the candle in a crystal holder flickered, throwing the planes of Tom's face into shadow, highlighting his prominent cheekbones. His gray eyes reflected the golden light.

"Don't look now," she said, "but heads turned all over this restaurant, and there was a definite hush when we walked into the room. We're making history here."

"The hush and head turning was everyone looking at the most beautiful woman in Texas."

"Stop it!" she exclaimed, laughing. "We're getting stared at right now, and the report of our dinner together will be all over Royalton County before the hour is up."

"If that's the case, let's give them reason to gossip," he said, moving the candle out of his way. He reached across the table to slip his hand behind her head and draw her toward him while he leaned forward to kiss her.

The instant she knew what he intended, she started to protest. At the same time amusement bubbled in her.

As his mouth covered hers, she was lost with longing, remembering his sexy, bone-melting kiss from this morning. When his tongue touched hers, her heart thudded.

Desire kindled, a burning flame low inside her. She wanted him, and every contact reaffirmed her longing.

Gathering her wits, she caught his wrist in her hand and pulled away, glancing into his eyes to see pinpoints of searing hunger that made her heart pound even more.

"Now you've really done it," she said as he sat back and replaced the candle.

He gave her a level, satisfied look, but it held a promise of things to come and was as sexy as his kiss. She tore her gaze from his and looked down at her hands in her lap, trying to act cool, regain her composure and dredge up some resistance to his seductive ways.

To her relief, a waiter arrived. Rose passed on the glass of wine Tom offered, instead drinking only water, while he ordered a glass of white wine.

"Well, you did give everyone enough gossip to carry them through the rest of the month. It'll be all over West Texas, not just the county by morning. This old feud is very well-known."

"Maybe it'll be clear to one and all that we've declared a truce."

"I don't think you've left one shred of doubt involving reconciliation," she remarked drily, and they both laughed.

"The Devlin-Windcroft peace agreement may worry whoever's behind the incidents at the ranch. With that in mind, I considered trying to keep our dinner together a secret and taking you somewhere else. There are advantages either way. If everyone knows that we're no longer fighting, the criminal may be more careful or lie low for a time."

"Well, it's too late now if you don't want people to know."

"True." Their beverages arrived and as soon as they were alone, Tom raised his glass in a salute. "May all our moments together be unforgettable."

She couldn't resist touching her glass to his with a faint clink.

"I'm glad you talked Daddy into letting go of the feud," she said, trying to steer the conversation to less personal subjects.

"Someone is trying to stir hatred between Devlins and Windcrofts—unless the crimes have been a smoke screen for what that person really wants."

Glancing beyond her, Tom stood.

"Don't get up," came a brittle voice, and Rose turned to see tall blond Gretchen Halifax smiling at Tom. The city councilwoman glanced at Rose. "Evening, Rose. I didn't know you two knew each other," Gretchen said to Tom. "I can't believe my eyes and I'm surprised Earl Finlay from the Royal newspaper isn't in here. A Devlin sitting at the same table with a Windcroft? Is it possible? I would have said no, except I'm looking at both of you."

"We have made peace between the families," Tom said.

Gretchen's laughter made heads turn. "It looks to me as if you've bounced from hate to love," she said, flicking another cold look at Rose before turning back to Tom.

"I'm sure you're on the campaign trail, so to speak, here in town," Tom remarked. "Election time for the office of mayor is almost here."

"I do hope I have your support. Rose, you've probably lived away long enough that you can't vote anyway, can you?"

"That's right," Rose answered and instantly lost any of Gretchen's attention as the councilwoman turned fully to Tom. While the two talked, Rose studied Gretchen. She was attractive enough in her own way with her pale blond hair in a smooth chignon. She was slender and shapely, yet, to Rose, too severe and as cold as ice.

"I'm interrupting your cozy little dinner," Gretchen said, "but I had to come over and see for myself that you two actually are on speaking terms. I hope this isn't a show for some hidden reason."

"Our sitting here together is for real," Tom replied easily. "I enjoy Rose's company."

"Well, I'll leave you two alone. Now don't forget to vote," Gretchen said and moved on, pausing two tables away to greet more people. In a few minutes she joined a distant relative of the Devlins, Malcolm Durmorr.

"I guess a man has succumbed to Gretchen's charms," Rose observed. "There's Malcolm Durmorr with her."

"Yes. That's one Devlin that Uncle Lucas doesn't want to claim. Malcolm has done shady things in his past and been on the wrong side of the law. From what I've heard, he's always after easy money. He and Gretchen are strange bedfellows. She seems damned ambitious."

"Actually he doesn't look too happy with her right now." Rose turned away when Malcolm glanced at her, his small brown eyes reminding her of a lizard.

"I think they may be discussing us," Tom said. "Probably speculating about the feud ending and what that'll mean."

"Daddy wonders if Malcolm is mixed up in Jonathan's murder. And my family would all agree with you that Malcolm is a nefarious sort."

"Your father might not be far off in his suspicions," Tom said. "It isn't out for the public, but it looks as if

Jonathan Devlin died from an overdose of potassium chloride, not from natural causes as first thought. Problem is, potassium chloride poisoning is damned difficult to trace. Whoever did it had to know how to give him the shot."

"All of you Texas Cattleman's Club guys, including Sheriff O'Neal, were suspicious of Nita for a while. She would never do anything to someone," Rose said.

"I'm sure she wouldn't. She's not a suspect now."

"Malcolm worked as an orderly a long time ago," Rose said, rubbing her arms. "I remember because at the time, I thought I wouldn't want to be in a hospital and have him touch me. There's something creepy about the man."

"You're right on all counts."

"You and Connor and your other Cattleman's Club friends are considering Malcolm as a suspect in Jonathan's killing, aren't you?"

Tom gave her a level look, and she smiled. "All right. Don't answer me. I don't need to know and I'm sure what all of you do is confidential, given out only to wives. Enough talk on the subject of Malcolm, as well as Gretchen who didn't bother to say goodbye to me when she found out I can't vote. May Jake Thorne be our next mayor."

"Amen to that one," Tom said.

At that moment their waiter served their tossed green salads and their conversation drifted to other topics. As the meal progressed, and in spite of delicious pink grilled salmon dinners, Tom seemed as indifferent to eating as she was.

"The evening is still early. Let's go to the Royalton to one of the lounges where we can dance," he suggested, and she had to laugh.

"You do like to live dangerously. There will be no stopping the rumors about the Windcrofts and Devlins."

"What are we waiting for?" he asked, standing. "I knew when I met with your father that I was making history."

Eagerly Rose left with him and they drove the short distance on Main to Royal's oldest and finest hotel. Tom held her arm as they crossed the quiet lobby, with its potted palms, plush Oriental carpets and high ceilings. They went to a dimly lit lounge where a band was playing, and anticipation made her pulse accelerate. Tom led her to an empty booth in a secluded corner near the dance floor, where she asked once again for water while he ordered a beer.

When he asked her to dance, she went to the dance floor and into his arms, letting go of her worries and simply enjoying the moment.

Slow-dancing to old favorites heaped another coal on the fires of seduction. As she moved in perfect unison with him, her desire burned hotter. "It's like we've done this forever instead of only one time before," she said.

"I've dreamed about you," he said. "Catching the first glimpse of you when I was on the road this morning, I was stunned."

"Your surprise wasn't one iota greater than mine," she admitted, gazing up into his thickly lashed eyes. "I never expected to see you at our farm. I would have been surprised to see you anywhere in Texas. When I saw you at the conference, you were leaving the country. What project are you working on now? If I remember correctly, the last one was in Madrid."

"I finished in Madrid and am letting others run things so I can take a long leave. I meant to get your phone number, but I got called away from the conference by an emergency."

"I had to leave early, too. I intended to see you again," she said. After a moment she asked, "Are you getting tired of the demolition business?"

"No, I like it. It's just that I feel at home in Texas. The ranch I've acquired is only thirty miles from Uncle Lucas's place. I want to live out here and raise cattle and I'll have my uncle to turn to for advice. And now, Rose, I can be near you."

"Only as long as I'm here. This is temporary until the trouble stops. I don't want to stay here. Growing up, I couldn't wait to get away from the farm," Rose replied, disturbed again to learn how close to her family he soon would live.

"I want the peace and quiet of living away from the city and I need a new pursuit. There are constant challenges in ranching. Plus I want to stay close to Uncle Lucas and my cousins."

"I'm surprised you're interested."

"Relatives here are important to me, and this is my blood family. I keep in touch with two foster families I lived with while I was growing up."

"The Devlins have a long history, just as the Windcrofts do," she remarked, wondering when and how to break the news to Tom about the baby.

"From what I understand, old Jonathan Devlin was the family patriarch as well as the town historian. He must have been a powerful personality. When my mother found out she was pregnant out of wedlock, she fled to California rather than face her grandfather's ire. At birth she gave me up for adoption."

Rose chilled, seeing a parallel to her own pregnancy

and knowing she would never give up her baby willingly. At the same time she was thankful her father had been loving and accepting. "Did you ever know your father's identity?"

Tom shook his head, and she felt as if a wall had just risen between them. "My blood mother was Annawyn. My blood father was unknown. She never told even Lucas."

"How did you go from adoption to foster homes?"

"My adoptive parents were killed in a car accident. My foster experiences were good, but it's not the same as your own family. I'm glad to have found Uncle Lucas. Anyway, that's the past," Tom said and his tone lightened. He pulled her closer to him, and she was keenly aware of her legs brushing against his while they danced. "Now Uncle Lucas has gotten interested in family history. He's behind having Jonathan's house restored."

"Nita told me. Then the historic site is going to be donated to Royal."

"My uncle and cousins are great. And because I came here to spend time with them, I found you again." When Tom looked down at her, his gaze warmed.

"I'm here because I worry about Nita and Daddy. Too many bad things have happened. When I was in Dallas, I couldn't get them off my mind."

"I worry about you out there in the guesthouse alone. Someone is dead set on hurting the Windcrofts, and at least Connor is in the main house where he can guard Nita and your father. I'd say you're vulnerable where you are."

"Since I haven't lived here for a long time, I don't feel like I'm involved," she said, her gaze lowering to his mouth while she remembered how it felt to have his lips on hers.

"You're a Windcroft, so you're at risk. You need to be careful, too," he said, his gaze roaming over her features while she mulled over his warning.

"All of you are so closemouthed about your Cattleman's Club, but I know that Nita sought your help involving the farm."

"So far, no one has turned up anything." Tom's breath fanned her ear and tickled her.

"Rose," he murmured. "I want you naked in my arms."

She inhaled, looking up at him. "I lost myself that weekend. I don't usually act so impulsively." She knew she had an opening to tell him about her pregnancy, but the words wouldn't come.

He gave her a look that tangled her thought processes. "I'm glad you were impulsive. That was one of the best weekends I've ever had."

Before she could answer, the music changed to a fast number. They moved apart and continued to dance. After two more numbers he shed his coat.

At midnight she caught his hand. "I need to go home. It's getting late, and by the time we drive back to the farm, it'll be really late."

"Sure," he said, taking her arm to leave. As soon as they were in the car, they rode in silence for a few minutes. Rose's thoughts were on her need to admit the truth to Tom. Reluctance still filled her as they left Royal. Avoiding the issue, she turned in the seat to watch him drive.

"Tell me some more about your business. How did you get into demolition?" she asked.

"I got a baseball scholarship to college, where I majored in engineering. I was fascinated by the science of demolition but put it aside when I graduated and went with the pros." As he answered her, he adjusted the rear-view mirror.

"You're that Tom Morgan of baseball?" she asked in surprise. "I don't follow the games, but I've heard your name," she said, realizing that explained why he was so fit and muscular.

"After baseball I returned to my other interests and started my own demolition contracting firm," Tom continued, yet she suspected his attention wasn't fully on their conversation and her concern grew. The night seemed to close in and the darkness held hidden threats. She knew her imagination was taking leaps and she reminded herself that they were safe in a locked car, still in Royal.

"I am really looking forward to moving to this ranch. I want you to go with me to look at the land I've bought."

She took a deep breath, realizing how entwined their lives were becoming whether she wanted it or not. The thought that control over her life was slipping away from her disturbed her.

"A ranch will be a welcome challenge," he replied, glancing again in the rearview mirror, and she turned to look over her shoulder at the traffic behind them.

"And you like challenges most of the time," she said, thinking she hadn't been one. She had melted in his arms and succumbed to his seductive charm instantly.

"I like some contests but not all," he replied too solemnly while he continued to glance into the rearview mirror.

"You're watching to see if we're being followed, aren't you?" she asked as a chill slithered down her spine.

Four

Rose looked over her shoulder. "Do we have someone tailing us?" she repeated, unable to imagine that she would be involved in what had been happening at the farm.

"No, but I don't want to be caught unawares."

Neither did she, and it was a relief when they passed through the gates of the horse farm. She relaxed as Tom drove to the guesthouse. When he unlocked and held open her door, she looked up at him. She hadn't wanted to rush things, but she also didn't want the night to end. She had enjoyed being with him, and it seemed too soon to say goodbye.

"Want to come in?" she asked, once again knowing she was taunting a tiger and going to bring more trouble on herself. "You can have a glass of wine or a cup of coffee—whichever you prefer. Or hot chocolate, which is what I like at bedtime."

"You know what I like at bedtime?" he asked in a husky voice, following her inside, then closing and locking the door.

"I don't think I want to find out," she said, moving ahead of him toward her kitchen. "What would you like to drink?"

"I'll take hot chocolate with you," he said, catching up to her in long strides and taking her arm. "I know I'm being overprotective, but let me go into the kitchen first," he suggested.

"Oh, surely everything is all right. We have an alarm system and lights. Connor has men patrolling the place at night."

"Indulge me and let me check out the house," Tom said with a finality that ended her argument. When he went ahead of her to switch on lights and look around, it occurred to her that he might be armed. Another chill slid down her spine, but then she shrugged it away. It seemed absurd to think she could be in danger. Yet she knew it was possible. Nita had been through something similar and Rose knew how shocked Nita had been when bad things had started happening.

Tom moved around the room, looking in the pantry, then the utility room. Finally he motioned her into the kitchen. "You fix the drinks while I continue to look around."

When he left, she gazed out a window at the dark night that had never bothered her before. Now the darkness held a potential for evil, and she closed the wooden shutters.

In minutes she had prepared steaming mugs of hot

chocolate. When Tom returned, he had shed his coat and tie, unbuttoned his collar and rolled back his sleeves.

"Our chocolate is ready and I've got a plate of cookies. We can take them into the other room and build a fire," Rose said.

He took the tray holding the cups and plate from her and carried it into the large living area, where he put it down and crossed the room to start a fire. While he did, she switched on the stereo to familiar old favorites. As soon as the fire was roaring, Tom turned around. Rose sat on the leather sofa, expecting him to join her. Instead he walked around the room switching off the lamps, so the only light was from the blazing fire and the golden glow that spilled from the hall.

As he approached her, Rose's heart thudded. One look into his smoky eyes and she knew he intended to kiss her.

"Come here," he said, taking her hand and pulling her to her feet.

Her common sense said to protest and step away, but words wouldn't come and she wanted to kiss him.

"Since I walked through the front door at seven," he said as he wrapped her in his embrace, "I've exhibited endless patience, because I've wanted to be here with you in my arms. That quick kiss in the restaurant was torment. I wanted so much more." Placing both hands on either side of her head, he combed his fingers into her hair. "I don't think you want to say goodbye. Right now your pulse is racing just as mine is. You sound as breathless as I feel," he said, brushing light kisses on her temple. He tilted her head up to look into her eyes and when he did, a riveting gray devoured her. His eyes were thickly lashed, impossible to withstand. Why was she so susceptible to his charm, so easily seduced by him?

Her pulse pounded and her mouth went dry. She slid her arms around his neck. She wanted him with all her being and she knew she was asking for trouble by the wagonload. She should get him out of her life until she was ready to inform him of her pregnancy.

But desire was a hot flame, a need that drove everything else out of mind. As he leaned down to kiss her, she stood on tiptoe. Their tongues clashed and his went deep into her mouth, stroking and sending ripples of erotic feelings that heightened her longing.

"Ah, Rose," he said. "How I've wanted you and dreamed of you. I want my hands and my tongue all over you."

His words carried their own caresses while his hand went to her zipper, and cool air brushed her shoulders as he peeled away her dress. They were near the fire, and its warmth spilled over her but was nothing compared to the heat that Tom stirred.

When she unbuttoned his shirt and pushed it off his shoulders, her fingers shook with urgency. He tossed away his shirt and she unfastened his belt.

Bending down, Tom planted kisses from the corner of her mouth, along her ear and down her throat. His large hands cupped her breasts. She closed her eyes as his every touch rocked her. With a flick of his fingers he unfastened the clasp to her lacy black bra and tossed it aside.

"Darlin', you're gorgeous. You take my breath," he said, cupping her breasts and circling her taut nipples with his thumbs, lazy circles that tormented and teased. "Do you like that?" he asked. "Say it. Tell me you like it."

"You know I like what you're doing," she gasped, barely able to talk.

He took her nipple in his mouth, biting so lightly,

only enough to heighten her response, and then his tongue leisurely stroked the taut bud.

Desire was a scalding ache low inside her. She wanted him with all her being, had yearned for him for too long now. She shut her mind to the future and feasted on the present.

When he unzipped his trousers, they fell around his ankles. In a flash he shed his shoes, socks and white briefs, and she inhaled as her gaze roamed over his muscled body and strong legs, his hard masculinity.

Taking his stiff rod in her hand, she knelt to caress him, and then her tongue played with him until he groaned and slipped his hands beneath her arms, hauling her to her feet.

He gathered her into his embrace for a kiss that poured out the depth of his need and made her tremble with awe that he could want her so much.

How she desired him! She stroked his thick manhood until he picked her up and laid her on the rug in front of the fire. Watching her, he moved between her thighs, putting her legs over his shoulders to give him access to her as, with his tongue, he delved in her most intimate places.

She moaned, holding his strong arms, moving her hips, wanting more of him. "Tom, come here," she cried.

He stretched out beside her, taking her into his arms and lavishing kisses on her throat and ear, letting his hand drift down between her legs, his fingers going where his tongue had been as he began to caress her, igniting fires that engulfed her in sensation.

While her hips thrashed and a blinding need built, she clung to him.

"Tom!" she cried, nipping his shoulder, fondling his

thick manhood, lost to his touch and the passion that consumed her. "Tom, I want you."

Release burst in her, but only sufficient to intensify her need for all of him. She pushed him down and straddled him, running her hands over his magnificent body, admiring his powerful, well-sculpted muscles. Her fingers tangled in his black chest hair and then drifted lower.

When she trailed kisses on his chest, licking his nipples, moving down across his flat belly, his hands wound in her hair and he groaned. She ran her tongue along his thick rod while her fingers went between his legs to cup him and stroke lightly.

Wanting him more than ever, she turned him over to trace kisses along his smooth, muscled back. Her fingers played with his firm bottom before she continued lower, her hands running over the backs of his thighs, the short black hairs tickling her palms. He rolled over, and she took him in her mouth, her tongue licking him with slow deliberation.

With a groan he moved away. She watched him pick up his trousers and remove a condom. Unable to let him go, she stood and wrapped herself around him, pressing against his backside while her hands played with him and she kissed his nape.

He turned to pick her up and carry her back to the rug in front of the fire. As soon as he put her down, her hips shifted with need. She desired him desperately and held out her arms, sitting up to pull him to her.

"Come here. I want you," she said, showering kisses on him, letting her hands roam over him. When she spread her legs, he moved between them, pausing to put on the condom, then he lowered himself, entering her.

She cried out, arching to meet him, moving wildly.

She wrapped her long legs and her arms around him. Plunging deeply, his thick rod pulsed in her.

Gyrating in an age-old dance, Tom slowed, withdrawing as she gasped. "Tom, love me!" she cried.

Her hands clutched his bottom, and her legs tightened around him. Arching her back, she tried to pull him closer.

He thrust slowly into her again, an exquisite torment that drew out pleasure until she thought she would dissolve. She knew from his movements when his control was gone. He made love with her, ramming hard and fast, making her writhe in abandon.

As tension built, her world was only Tom. Lights behind her eyelids blinded her, and the sounds in her ears roared, shutting out all other noise.

Clinging to him tightly, she spasmed with release, pressing against him as rapture spilled over her. Tom plunged into her again and cried out, a deep primordial cry of need. He called her name, but she could barely hear him for her hammering pulse.

As they clung tightly to each other, their rhythm ebbed and they both tried to catch their breath.

His breathing was as ragged as hers, and she could feel their hearts beating in unison. Tom turned to brush light kisses on her temple.

Holding her against his heart, Tom rolled onto his side, taking her with him. He shifted so he could look at her while he combed damp locks away from her face. "You're fantastic," he said.

"I could say the same," she answered in euphoria, brushing feathery kisses on him in return, still running her hands over him and relishing his hard muscles and his body given to her to enjoy.

"I've thought about you constantly," he admitted, and she looked at him in surprise.

"Go on!" she exclaimed. "I don't believe you!"

"It's true. Why would I make up a thing like that?"

"To sweet-talk me into more seduction," she said, smiling at him. She moved against him sensuously in a slow shift of her body.

"You little witch! Give me some rest," he said.

She laughed. "As if you gave me any in the past hour."

He kissed her, a binding kiss that sealed their union and proclaimed how good things were between them.

"I don't think I can stand," he said. "You've demolished me."

"Stop complaining," she replied. "You loved every passionate second of it, and before I know it, you'll be trying to get me to do the same things to you all over again."

"Sure, I will. I hope I can talk you into doing them over and over all night long." He framed her face with his hands. "You'll never know how much I've wanted you," he said in a deep, gravelly voice.

"And after the past hour, don't you think I desired you equally as much?"

"Couldn't possibly," he said. "You can't imagine the way I need you in my arms, in my bed."

"Instead here we are on my floor. Thank goodness I have privacy out here."

He grinned and stood, then bent down to pick her up.

"Tom! If we're going to the bedroom, I can walk." Ignoring her protest, he scooped her into his arms easily and headed toward her bedroom. He let her switch on a light, then he carried her into the big bathroom, where he set her on her feet while he filled the marble tub with steaming water.

Rose added bath oil and lit some tall candles. Tom climbed in and took her hand to help her, and she sat between his legs, settling her back against him. "This is the way a bath should be taken," she said, running her fingers along his thigh, feeling the short hairs on his legs.

He soaped her leisurely, the textured washcloth an erotic roughness on her breasts. Then his fingers went between her legs to touch her. He wrapped his legs around hers, spreading her legs with his, giving his fingers access to her. In minutes a fire rekindled in her as if she hadn't been satisfied only a short time before.

She twisted around to slide over him. He was hard and ready, hungry for her. When she leaned close to kiss him, her breasts rubbed his chest. Soon she pulled away from the kiss and settled on his thick, hard rod, closing her eyes.

She moved her hips, pumping while his hips rose. Her hands played with his nipples and she tilted her head back, closing her eyes, savoring the feelings once again.

His hands toyed with her breasts. His skin was like hers, hot, wet and slippery, water gleaming on his brawny muscles. He thrust forcefully, crying her name. "Rose, Rose."

She came, release bringing ecstasy again, and she felt him achieve his climax. He gave a throaty growl before enveloping her in his hug.

Satiated and exhausted, she fell on him, draping her arms over his shoulders and kissing the corner of his mouth. He turned his head to give her another one of those satisfied kisses that proclaimed she was his woman.

They finished bathing, dried and went to bed wrapped in each other's arms. They made love again, showering together afterward.

Finally at half past four she ran her fingers along his jaw, feeling the stubble. "You better get up and go home. My daddy is old-fashioned, and if you stay until morning, we might find our lives really complicated."

"All right," Tom said, rolling out of bed. Stretching leisurely, she slipped on a robe, then followed him to the living area, where she watched him dress, cherishing every moment and knowing what she needed to do. She accompanied him to the back door.

In the kitchen Tom faced her, resting one hand on her shoulder. "Go to breakfast with me today. Let me pick you up at seven. If that's too soon, we can make it later."

"I'm accustomed to eating early. My stepmother, Jane, serves promptly at seven, and you better be there while the food is hot." Rose thought about the day and the work she had waiting. "Unfortunately I can't. I have a brochure and logo for a real-estate company that I have to get out."

"How about lunch or dinner?" He waited, one finger hooked over his shoulder holding his coat and tie, his shirt unbuttoned to his navel and revealing his chest hair and muscles.

"Tom, I don't want to get too deeply involved," she said with a pounding heart. An inner voice screamed at her to tell him about her pregnancy now, but she couldn't get out the words. "I need a breather," she said swiftly, hoping she sounded firm. He didn't look like the type of man to beg a woman to see him. When his lips curled, she experienced both relief and regret. A lot of regret that she didn't want to deal with right now.

"That's usually my speech, darlin'. I guess I deserve to have someone say it to me. If that's what you want, that's what we'll do. You almost told me that at the beginning of the evening, didn't you?"

She nodded. "Sorry, Tom."

"Don't be sorry. Last night was great, and if you change your mind and want to go out, let me know."

"I had a wonderful time," she said.

"So did I, darlin'. I'll miss you." When she reached for lights in the back entryway, he caught her hand. "Leave it dark and let me look around first."

"You're scaring me with your precautions."

"Good. You need to be careful. Just don't forget—you're a Windcroft, you're involved. Anyone on this place is at risk." All the time he was talking, he was looking at the drive and yard, which were well lit with outside lighting.

"'Bye, darlin'," he said, slipping his arm around her waist and pulling her to him to kiss her in a long, passionate, possessive kiss that curled her toes and stopped her breathing. And filled her with more regret.

When he released her, he smiled, turned and left. She watched his long strides as he walked to his car and knew he was walking right out of her life.

She had asked him to, but it still hurt. Deep inside, she had a knot of guilt and uneasiness. She should tell him about her pregnancy soon, but she needed space and distance before she could deal with him.

She watched him drive away. With a sigh she closed the back door. Shivering, she rubbed her arms, feeling alone. Should she continue to go out with him so they had a chance to fall in love?

She knew the answer was no because all too soon, when she revealed her pregnancy, he would want to marry her. She was certain he was the type to feel obligated.

She switched off lights and went to bed, lying in the dark and remembering being in Tom's arms, being loved by him. She'd had a wonderful time—but duty couldn't serve in place of love, and she wanted a marriage of love. She was certain to the depths of her being that Tom wouldn't wait to give love a chance but would want to marry her immediately when he learned she was pregnant with his child.

Tom drove along the driveway, watching the swath of road that was revealed in his headlights, as well as glancing into the darkness on either side of the car, wondering if all was safe on the Windcroft land.

When he returned to the Devlins' D Bar V Ranch, he passed the sprawling one-story brick-and-frame ranch house. In the lush green lawn surrounding the house, automatic sprinklers sprayed silver arcs of water, creating an oasis in cactus and mesquite country.

Dark shadows were broken by splashes of light from lamps on tall posts along the drive as he headed for the guesthouse.

Once inside and reaching his bedroom, Tom stripped and sprawled on the bed, unable to sleep for thinking about Rose.

If she wanted to break it off between them, he could. He had always known that a day would come when a woman would tell him to get out of her life before he was ready to walk away on his own, and it finally had happened.

He wasn't happy that she wanted to stop seeing him, but he would get over it and the time would come when it wouldn't matter. They didn't have a commitment or anything serious between them. He hadn't been into obligations or long-term relationships and now he'd met a woman who wasn't either.

"Serves you right," he said aloud to himself. In any affair he had always been the one to walk. So she was the first this time—it wouldn't matter. Sooner or later he would have wanted out. So why was he unhappy about it and unable to sleep?

He groaned and switched his thoughts to the danger that surrounded the Windcrofts. Rose really shouldn't be alone in the guesthouse. Tom was certain about that. She was far more vulnerable than she realized.

He needed to call a Cattleman's Club meeting to let them know about the truce between the Windcrofts and the Devlins. Sheriff O'Neal had asked his fellow club members for aid and, along with the sheriff, there were five of them working on solving Jonathan Devlin's murder and trying to find who was behind the terrible things that had been happening at the Windcroft place.

Mulling over the facts, Tom tossed and turned, but in too short a time he was back to thinking about Rose, admitting to himself that he didn't want to break things off with her.

After three hours of fitful sleep he woke, showered and then called everyone to set a meeting at noon at the club. He then made arrangements at the club for a private room and lunch.

He went about his usual morning routine with his mind on Rose, no closer to a resolution.

At midday Tom drove into Royal, passing Pine Valley, the exclusive gated area where he had purchased a condo even though he had only slept in it one night before Lucas had insisted Tom stay on the Devlin ranch. Driving along Main, Tom gazed with satisfaction at his hometown that was built first by ranching and then oil money. Royal had boutiques, expensive shops, elegant homes. It was a bustling community of wealthy citizens, one he was proud to call home. Campaign signs were scattered along Main, some for Gretchen Halifax, others proclaiming Jake Thorne's campaign slogan—Thorne for Mayor: A Leader for Tomorrow.

Tom entered the sprawling, exclusive gentlemen's club established nearly ninety years ago by Henry "Tex" Langley. Tom liked the friends he'd made in the club, as well as the opportunity to be of service to others.

As he strode through a vast, high-ceilinged, dark-paneled room filled with heavy leather furniture and a fire blazing in the massive fireplace, he looked at rows of oil paintings, animal heads and antique guns decorating the walls. Maybe the Western heritage in his blood was what had given him an early interest in guns; he had his own collection, including some antiques.

He was shown to the private room he had reserved, where another fire blazed in the hearth. All of the men had already gathered, and Tom greeted each swiftly, accepting congratulations on ending the feud. Sheriff Gavin O'Neal's brown eyes held an unmistakable hint of uneasiness, and Tom braced for bad news.

Five

"All right, Gavin, what's the grim outlook?" Tom asked.

"Before you arrived, we talked about what we can do to move the investigation forward. It's obvious that we need to figure out some way to flush the killer into revealing himself."

"The majority of us decided that we need a decoy," Mark Hartman added.

"And I don't think so," Connor snapped, his blue eyes flashing fire.

"Sounds like a plan with possibilities. Something needs to be done before one of the Windcrofts gets hurt worse. So where will we get a decoy?" Tom asked, looking at solemn faces.

"We ask Rose," Gavin replied, and Tom's insides knotted. His first reaction was refusal, but before he could voice his opinion, Connor spoke.

"I'm against it. I say no," Connor repeated. "I don't think we should put her in harm's way."

"She's already in it," Gavin said. "Dammit, all the Windcrofts are. Y'all know they are."

For a moment the argument swirled around the room while Tom sat and listened to the myriad reasons for and against Rose trying to entice the killer.

"What would make Rose a decoy—even if she agreed to do it?" Tom asked.

"Gavin and I talked this over before you arrived," Jake replied. "If Jessamine Golden's treasure is the reason for all that's been happening to the Windcrofts, we let word get out that Rose knows where the gold is hidden. The killer will come after anyone who knows the location of it."

Chilled, Tom thought about the risk their plan would put Rose in. His inclination was still a firm refusal, but he thought of the alternatives and the danger threatening the Windcrofts.

"Any event to move us closer to catching whoever is behind the killing and the multiple disasters is progress," Jake argued.

"We need to stir the murderer to reveal himself," Gavin said, supporting Jake. "The longer this drags on without the killer being discovered, the more at risk the Windcrofts are. Rose would be the perfect decoy."

"And I say she wouldn't," Conner argued stubbornly. "Let Nita be the decoy. She's tough and I'll be there to protect her."

"Nita is in the main house with you and her father and stepmother. She's too protected," Jake argued.

"That's right," Gavin added and looked at Tom.

"Tom, we want you to ask Rose if she'll be a decoy and we're asking you to stay with her to guard her."

"What do you think about it?" Jake asked. "We've already decided you're the one to get the most involved."

"Don't rush it," Connor told his brother quietly, both of them looking at Tom, and the clash of wills between the two brothers was palpable.

Tom gazed around the room at all the men who were watching him. "All your arguments are valid," he replied solemnly.

"Connor, remember Rose's life may be in jeopardy anyway," Jake insisted. "You can't ignore that the incidents have gotten progressively worse."

"I don't want Rose to be a decoy," Tom said. "But Jake's right. Either way, her life's at stake. We all know that the sooner we catch the killer, the better. If I can protect her and we can get the killer to reveal himself, then that's the best solution."

"And it could be the quickest," Mark added.

"I want to ask Rose," Tom continued, looking around at each man again. "If she says no, then that's it. We don't try to persuade her to do it."

"I still say it should be Nita," Connor argued with a flushed face.

Tom shook his head. "As much as I'd like to agree with you, the guys are right. Nita is too protected and everyone knows she lives in the main house. Just as our killer probably knows that Rose is alone in the guest-house. If she agrees, then I'll stay with her, but I prefer to try to keep from being seen by anyone outside of the family and you guys."

"I agree," Gavin said. "The fewer people who know Rose has protection, the more likely our plan is to succeed."

"If someone has been doing all of this mischief to get the Windcroft land in hopes of finding the treasure, then he won't be able to resist going after Rose," Gavin said, and Tom's dislike of the plan deepened.

"We should be able to guard her enough that no one can get to her," Logan stated quietly, and the men all looked at each other. "With the backgrounds we have in this room—Special Ops, ranching, firefighting, demolition, self-defense, and Gavin is a sheriff—we should be able to give her all the protection she could possibly need," Logan added.

Gavin nodded. "I agree. But what's important is will Rose agree?"

"None of you have convinced me. I still don't think we ought to put her in that spot," Connor said gravely, refusing to relinquish his argument, and Tom sensed that Connor wasn't leveling with all of them, yet he couldn't imagine why not.

"She's an innocent in this," Connor persisted. "She's not accustomed to a rough-and-tumble world. If we set up Nita—and she probably would be willing—she can handle herself and we can protect her."

"With the exception of when she's with you, Nita doesn't get six steps from Will, from what you've told me," Jake said. "If it's Nita, we'll have to guard Will, too. I say it won't matter that Rose is no tomboy. That doesn't have anything to do with it. She doesn't have to be a muscled jock," Jake argued. "We'll guard her."

"I think we can fully protect her," Mark said quietly. "We can take shifts to relieve Tom of full responsibility."

"I'll call upon you guys when I need you," Tom said. Murmurs of agreement went around the room, but a muscle worked in Connor's jaw, strengthening Tom's gut feeling of something awry.

"All right, but if Rose says no, then it's no," Connor commanded, looking directly at Tom. "No arguments or fast-talk or pushing her into this."

"I agree," Tom replied, feeling his anxiety increase about protecting Rose.

"How do we get word out that Rose knows the location of the treasure?" Logan asked, and suggestions were made and rejected.

"How about I take Rose to lunch at the Royal Diner and let it slip in our conversation?" Tom asked. "If someone overhears us—which we can see to it that the people in the adjoining booths do—the news will be all over Royal within the hour."

"That's true," Mark stated. "If there is any place in this town where gossip spreads like wildfire, it's the Royal Diner."

Voices rose in assent and Tom agreed, but he couldn't shake a cold knot of worry concerning Rose. It didn't help his feelings to know that Connor was so intensely opposed to the plan. He couldn't decide whether it was his own trepidation or the influence of Connor, but Tom didn't feel right about what they were setting up.

"You're quiet, Tom," Gavin said.

"I'm thinking about Rose. I don't have a good feeling about this. It's too damned dangerous."

"I agree," Connor said.

"We've been over that and made a decision," Gavin stated.

"This ploy may make the killer tip his hand. It's up to Rose now," Mark said.

"If any one of us wanted to get to somebody, we could," Tom said.

"Again I agree with Tom," Connor said quietly.

With a nagging persistence Tom intuitively knew something was wrong as he gazed into Connor's inscrutable blue eyes. Why did he suspect Connor was holding back information? The Texas Cattleman's Club members had sworn to aid each other and to help save innocents' lives and traditionally they all confided in each other.

"Okay, if Rose agrees, how soon do we do this?" Gavin asked.

"Tom, you talk to Rose as soon as possible," Logan said. "I've got a feeling that something terrible will happen again soon. We need to find the killer before he kills again. Or even tries to and fails, like he did with Will Windcroft."

"All right, if Rose agrees, Tom will stay at the Windcroft place. Connor, you help him clear that with Will." Gavin turned to Tom. "Tom, you work it out with Rose. Are we agreed?"

Everyone consented, giving warnings and making more suggestions about things each one thought might help. Tom half listened while he contemplated approaching Rose. She wasn't going to like having him underfoot when she had given him his walking papers.

When the group began to disband, Tom glanced at Connor, determined to get to the source of what he was holding back.

"Before you go, Connor, will you wait up a minute? I'd like to talk to you."

"Yes, I will," Connor said in such clipped words that Gavin turned to look at both of them.

As soon as the two men were alone, Tom turned to Connor. "Something's bothering you."

"Yeah, it is, but a promise is a promise and I'm not at liberty to say what."

"I know it involves Rose."

"I've already said too much. I made a promise to Nita. Just guard Rose damned well and call me at the least hint of trouble. You'll do that, won't you?"

"Yes, I will," Tom answered solemnly. Connor brushed past him and strode out the door. Mystified, Tom trailed after him. What was the deep secret that made Connor adamantly opposed to setting Rose up as a decoy? She would have round-the-clock protection.

As Tom left the clubhouse, questions tormented him. Puzzled, he crossed the leaf-covered asphalt lot to his red pickup that was parked beneath an ancient mulberry tree. Broad shiny yellow leaves fluttered in the sunlight, but Tom didn't see the tree, the lot or the car.

He drove through downtown, his thoughts poring over what each man had said. Why would Connor volunteer Nita and argue so strongly that they couldn't use Rose? What was it about Rose that Connor was trying to shield?

Puzzled, Tom thought about Rose, her sleek body, her tummy that was rounded—something it hadn't been when he'd been with her before, five months earlier.

He turned to ice, freezing in the warm car. Stunned, Tom drove up on a curb, and it jolted him enough to pay attention to his driving. He pulled over to the curb. Was Rose pregnant with his child?

"I'll be damned!" he exclaimed aloud. It fit. If she was pregnant and she had shared the secret with her family, that would explain Connor's reluctance for Rose to be a decoy. Shocked, Tom thought about the possibility.

He remembered how she had refused his offer of a glass of wine at dinner last night. In Houston that first night, she'd had wine. Now that he thought more about it, her figure had definitely changed.

Rose could be pregnant with his child. If she was, she hadn't told anyone the father's identity—or at least Connor hadn't known, Tom was sure. Rose—pregnant! And her family knew. It fit everything that had happened in the past hour. He thought about Rose telling him she didn't want to see him again for a while.

Tom stared ahead without really seeing what was in front of him. He was awestruck with the knowledge that he was going to be a father. He had always wanted his own kids. Now he was going to have a baby with Rose. So far, everything he knew about Rose was good—she was intelligent, personable and capable or she wouldn't have her own successful business. She was deeply into family ties in spite of moving to Dallas, because when trouble had struck, she had moved her business home so she could help her family. From what he knew about Rose, she would be a good, caring mother. A baby with Rose. He guessed that had to be the reason for Connor's reluctance to place Rose at risk.

Tom thought again about Rose saying she didn't want to go out with him anymore. She was trying to get him out of her life. That hurt and angered him, yet at the same time he hadn't made any commitment to her. He had to face the truth that he hadn't given Rose any reason to trust that he would want to be in a child's life.

This wasn't what he had dreamed about—far from it. He had always thought that someday he would find one special woman who he could love and trust. They would have a family and he would try to be the best father he could possibly be.

Yet anger slowly mushroomed in him that she hadn't shared the news with him now that he was here in Royal. How long had she intended to withhold the truth? Had she thought she could keep it from him and go back to Dallas before he discovered she was carrying his child?

She wasn't going to tell him about their baby. *His* baby.

How could she keep that from him even one day? He condemned himself, but he hurt and blamed her, as well.

He backed up and swung the truck out, moving into traffic and now driving by rote. His mind was still on Rose. Questions, doubts, fears, anger and awe, contrasting emotions churned his insides. He clamped his jaw closed so tightly that it hurt.

They weren't in love—he knew that, but he had wanted to continue seeing her. He thought they had been good together, but that wasn't what she wanted. She didn't want to share their baby with him.

What if he had stayed in California and never learned the truth? Would he have ever known his own child?

His knuckles were white on the steering wheel. He eased his foot off the gas pedal, realizing he had left Royal and was almost at the vehicle's top speed.

He couldn't get his breath. Taking deep gulps of air, he changed lanes and pulled off the road onto a shoulder, hearing the grass swish against his tires. When he parked by the bar ditch, silence descended.

Every second of the past few minutes would be etched in his mind forever: the clear blue sky, the flat land covered with feathery mesquite, the rumble of traffic speeding along the highway, the crisp fall day.

He pulled out his cellular phone to call Rose.

The moment she answered, he was tongue-tied. He might be completely wrong.

"Rose, this is Tom. I need to see you as soon as possible." He finally got out the words.

"Sure. I can take a break anytime. Where are you now?"

"Driving back to the ranch. I'll go to the horse farm instead. I want to talk to you."

"Fine. I'll be waiting," she said and hung up.

Rose replaced the phone. Tom was coming to talk to her, and whatever he wanted to discuss must be some kind of emergency or something the Club members had decided. Nita had mentioned they'd planned a meeting for noon, and Rose knew Connor was increasingly worried that they hadn't caught the killer.

Rose hurried to her room to brush her hair. She shouldn't care that she was going to see Tom again, but she was unable to stop her pulse from accelerating. She straightened the house, shut down her computer and when she heard his truck, she hurried to the door.

As soon as he stepped from his vehicle, her pulse took another leap while she watched his long-legged stride cover the ground. Wind blew locks of his black hair away from his face. Her baby would have the most handsome man for a father.

When Tom crossed the porch, his searching gaze stabbed into her. She sucked in her breath in surprise because he looked upset.

"What's wrong? Has something else happened?" she asked.

"Let's go inside," he said. His words were clipped, his fists were clenched and his gray eyes had darkened.

Mystified, she entered the house. In the family room

she faced him. He placed his fists on his hips while his gaze raked over her in a blatant study that lingered on her stomach.

"You're pregnant, aren't you?" he asked bluntly.

Six

While Rose's heart thudded, she raised her chin and pulled herself together.

"Yes, I am, but that doesn't concern you," she said coolly.

"The hell with that! Why didn't you tell me?" Tom asked.

"You're not a part of my pregnancy. What I do doesn't pertain to you," she said, trying to maintain control, sound calm and hide the total panic that had seized her.

"I want to be involved. I know I haven't made any commitment or given you any reason to trust that I would want to be in our child's life, but that's because I didn't know you're having my baby. Well, I'm here to right that and to make a commitment."

She blinked, taken aback. "You're acting impulsively. You haven't talked about committing to anything."

"I'm ready to now. I know what I want. And you

didn't answer my question. Why didn't you tell me? You can't hide a pregnancy." His clean-shaven jaw jutted out and his expression was as formidable as his question.

"You didn't know when you left here this morning. How did you find out?" she asked, her sense of panic rising over her inability to control what was happening.

"For one reason, your body doesn't look exactly the same," he said.

She flushed and wound her fingers together. She couldn't argue with that answer.

"How could you do this?" he asked. "If I had stayed in California, you wouldn't have let me know, would you?"

"Eventually," she said, taking a deep breath. "All right, so you're going to be a father," she said tightly, hating that he had discovered the truth before she was ready to tell him herself. She'd wanted to tell him at a time that suited her best. She would have to deal with him immediately and make decisions she had intended to postpone.

"Will you marry me?" he asked.

She closed her eyes and rocked back on her heels. "I was certain that the minute you knew the truth, you would propose," she said, opening her eyes to meet his piercing gaze. "This is exactly why I didn't want to tell you. You're proposing when you know there's no love between us."

"Look, there can be caring and love and now there's reason to commit to each other. I want to help raise my child. I want a say in what happens. And, Rose, you and I need to give ourselves a chance. I'm willing to make a commitment."

"You're doing that for all the wrong reasons. You didn't feel this way last night."

He winced but shook his head. "I'm willing to have a long-term relationship."

"Just like that?" she exclaimed, snapping her fingers. "We're not in love. My answer to your proposal is no." She hated the way things were going between them and wished she had done this differently.

"You can't mean that," he said, all color draining from his face. He paled to the extent that she thought he might faint.

"Look, sit down before you fall down," she said, now worried about him and his reaction, yet feeling more strongly than ever that she didn't want to be pressured into a loveless marriage. "Hot sex isn't a basis for marriage."

"A baby is," he said, and his voice was cold steel that plunged her into a chill.

"I want to marry for love," she stated emphatically.

"Maybe that will come," he said. "I'm willing to give it a chance." He raked his fingers through his hair. Black locks sprang back, strands falling over his forehead. "I know I haven't made a commitment to you, but as far as I was concerned, we were headed toward seeing more of each other."

"Most men would be glad to shirk this responsibility. They would happily disappear."

"I'm not most men, and you're not going to ignore me or get rid of me. I won't let you walk away. I have rights."

"You're going to make this difficult," she said with a sigh.

"It doesn't have to be, but I will if it means getting

to be a father to my baby." He moved closer and put his hands on her shoulders. Even though he didn't hold her tightly, she was annoyed by his demands and spur-of-the-moment proposal.

"Take your hands off me!" she snapped, and he dropped his arms to his sides.

"I can take you to court and try to get joint custody," he reminded her.

She felt chilled and wondered if a big court battle with him might loom in her future. "I'm marrying for love and no other reason," she said flatly.

"You think about depriving our baby of a full-time loving father. You consider it long and hard, Rose, because if push comes to shove, I will take you to court and fight for joint custody," he said, his voice turning cold.

She blinked, certain this was no empty threat. He had the money to get a battery of high-powered lawyers, and there would be publicity because of his wealth. Sympathy would not be with her.

"You want to push us into a loveless marriage."

"Just give us a chance. And I'll guarantee you I'm going to love this baby and shower it with affection. I don't ever want my child to be deprived of a caring family. You might as well face the fact that we'll have to come to some agreements."

"You're already threatening to take my baby from me."

"I said joint custody. That's different. It's a legal process. You tried to keep your pregnancy from me, so don't even start about my taking your baby."

With her heart still pounding, she inhaled and gazed up at Tom. She always fought for control and hated when she didn't have command of a situation. This one had spiraled out of hand from the first moment she had discovered her pregnancy. At least he recognized the fact that he had never made a commitment to her. He couldn't expect her to come running to him with news of her pregnancy under those circumstances, and she was glad to know he was willing to admit his lack of responsibility.

"I wish you'd told me," he said quietly, and in that moment she hurt because she faced the truth in her heart—he had a right to know about his baby and she should have told him the first time she'd seen him at the farm.

"I was going to tell you soon."

"Oh, right," he said in a cynical tone that rekindled her anger.

"You said yourself that you hadn't made any commitment and now that you know, you're already trying to take charge," she retorted. "You're a strong man and accustomed to dominating situations. Well, I'm accustomed to being in command, too. I don't want to change that."

"You'll have to yield some of your control. I realize that I'll have to. And I'd say you've already lost some of it."

Remaining silent, she hated to acknowledge that he was right.

"Connor knows about your pregnancy, doesn't he?"

"Yes, but I asked my family to keep my secret until I had a chance to tell the father—you."

When Tom's face flushed, she knew his anger had returned, but he clamped his jaw closed and didn't say anything for a moment. He gave her another long, speculative appraisal. "Do you know what you're having?"

"A girl."

"A baby girl!" he exclaimed. "Wow," he said, his tone filling with so much awe, Rose was slightly taken aback. "A little girl," he repeated, all anger leaving his voice. "Rose, you have to let me into your life."

"I do not *have* to do any such thing," she said, but the wonder in his voice laid siege to her determination to make all decisions herself.

"Marry me and give love a chance," he urged quietly.

"You're asking out of a sense of obligation. And you've already told me that you've bought a ranch and that's where you want to settle. Well, no, thanks. I've spent my whole life trying to get off the horse farm. I'm not turning around and moving right back to a ranch. And there's a big difference between letting you into my life and marrying you."

As they stared at each other, she could see fire snapping in the depths of his eyes. A muscle worked in his jaw and his fists were clenched. He took a deep breath. "I'm not giving up my baby," he declared.

"And I'm not giving up my life as I want to live it." She could feel the clash of wills and she hurt. This really wasn't the way she'd wanted him to discover the truth.

He looked as if he were making an effort to calm down. "There's something else I have to tell you, so we might as well sit," he said.

"All right," she replied, wondering what else they had to discuss. She scooted back into a corner of the sofa and Tom sat close, turning to face her. He seemed to be mulling over what he intended to say.

"I don't even want to pass this on to you, but I'm obligated and if I don't, someone else will. The Texas Cattleman's Club members have a plan that involves you. I'll tell you right now that I oppose it completely."

Her curiosity rose. "Tell me what it is. It'll be my decision."

He frowned at her and leaned forward, placing his elbows on his knees. "We're asking you to be a decoy to draw out the killer."

"How on earth can I lure a murderer?" she exclaimed, surprised by his announcement.

"We let it be known that you've found the treasure."

"Of course!" she exclaimed, seeing at once how the strategy could work. "How would you get that rumor started?"

"Since I know you're pregnant, there's no way in hell I want you to put yourself at risk," he said, avoiding answering her question.

"Don't you think I'm in peril right now? Even without that rumor?"

He knotted his fists. "Dammit, yes, you are. That was the only reason I listened and considered letting you do this."

"There's no 'letting' me do it." If I want to do it, you can't stop me," she snapped and felt the tension increase between them. "Go ahead. Tell me the details."

He glared at her in silence. "I don't want you to do it," he insisted.

"So you said. But I want to hear what all of you have worked out."

Tom sighed. "The plan is for us to eat at the Royal Diner soon and make sure someone overhears us talking about you knowing the whereabouts of the treasure. You know how word travels and anything that happens in the diner goes all over town within hours."

"Maybe minutes," she remarked drily.

He thought a moment and nodded. "I'll stay with you to protect you, but we need to see to it that people don't know I'm here. And that means I'm with you around the clock. The others will come at the slightest notice, and Connor will be close."

"If you're with me, I'll have more protection than I do now."

"That's the reason Connor and I have given the scheme the slightest consideration."

"I want to do it because maybe the ruse will get this situation over and done with and everyone will be safe again. We might as well try. I know you'll be with me constantly, so I don't see how I can be in as much jeopardy as I am now."

"Common sense tells me you're right, but my gut feeling is bad. I don't want you in danger."

"I'd say it's settled about the plan."

"Now who's acting on impulse?" he snapped. "Think this over."

"I don't have to consider the ploy a long time. I think this is the best thing to do," she replied.

"Connor opposed this plan adamantly, and since learning the truth, I understand why."

"I hear your objections. Trust me, I do. But it's decided now that we'll try the plan. What's the first step?"

"Go to lunch at the Royal Diner."

"What if no one eavesdrops or overhears us? Maybe we'll have to do this several times."

"If there are some snoopy people who eat in the Royal Diner at noontime, the news will get around. Let's go to lunch tomorrow," he suggested. "If you're hell-bent to do this, there's no need in waiting."

"That's fine with me."

They stared at each other and she could feel the emotional tug-of-war between them.

"You can tell your family what we're going to do, although Connor probably will tell them before you've had a chance. And I want to talk to your father about our plans for you to be a decoy."

"Even if he doesn't like the idea, he'll do what I want. I think he'll agree it's the best solution."

"Also, I want to tell him that I intend to marry you. I won't have your family thinking I don't want to."

She nodded, hurting and feeling more control slipping away from her. They stared at each other and she felt locked in an impasse.

"We can work this out if we try," he said.

"I hope so," she answered, but at the moment the chances looked slim.

"Rose, think about my proposal," Tom said, his voice changing and his tone holding a gentle note. "It would be good to be married."

"You don't know that," she said, looking away.

"You don't know that it wouldn't be good," he fired back. "Think about it. We're doing great when we're together, and now there's a wonderful reason to stay together."

"You're beginning to sound like a hopeless romantic. You surprise me. There are so many differences between us," she said and his eyes narrowed.

"I'm willing to try to iron them out," he said.

She remained silent, because at this point the differences seemed monumental and set in concrete.

"I'll move in here right away. I need to leave for a while, but I'll be back for dinner. I'll try to slip in without being followed. I don't want anyone other than our Cattleman's Club guys, our families and hands to know I'm here."

"Do you think you can keep that a secret?"

"Should be able to if I'm not followed. Once we've eaten in town, I don't need to leave the ranch. We can meet at the diner tomorrow and when we leave, we can go our separate ways."

"I pray this works and we catch whoever has been trying to hurt us."

"I'll be back about seven," he said and she watched him walk out of the room. As he left, she remained where she was until she heard the door close behind him. She walked to the front door and watched him get into his truck while she thought about the changes in her life in the past hour—changes that might alter her future forever. Beneath his surprise and anger had been a genuine desire for the baby that she had never expected.

She shook her hair away from her face. Tom knew about the baby now. *Tom knows.* The knowledge hounded her. His discovery of the truth had been worse than she had expected, but that was because the news hadn't come from her.

"Tom," she whispered, wondering how long it would take him to get over his hurt. His proposal dangled before her, but she had absolutely no intention of marrying him and settling on a ranch. She would never compromise on that.

She went to the kitchen, getting out chocolate syrup and a bottle of milk, when she heard a knock at the front door. Rose hurried to open the door, wondering if Tom had returned, but it was Nita who came striding in.

"Come back to the kitchen," Rose invited. "I'm going to get a glass of chocolate milk. Would you like one?"

"No, thank you," Nita replied and followed Rose into the kitchen. Nita put her hands on her hips while she surveyed Rose. "Are you all right?"

"I'm fine," Rose answered, filling a glass full of milk, then adding chocolate syrup.

"You can buy that already mixed," Nita said and Rose smiled.

"I know you can, but I like this. You're missing something by not having any."

"Not today. I saw Tom's pickup, so I assumed he came to tell you about the Cattleman's Club guys' plan."

"Yes, he did."

"Connor told me about their scheme to make you a decoy," Nita said. "Connor and Tom were opposed to setting you up as bait but finally agreed to go along. Rose, why don't you let me be the decoy?"

Rose shook her head. "No. There's no need. I'll be guarded constantly. Hopefully the killer won't know Tom is staying with me and it'll seem easy to get to me. Thanks, Nita, but let me do this."

"None of us want you to, but if you back out, you'll have to let more people know about your pregnancy."

"And I'm sure not ready to do that yet. I'm the decoy. Let's leave it at that."

"Are you absolutely sure it's all right with you? I know Daddy's not going to like it one bit."

"I think it's a good idea. None of us is safe now. Let's see if we can't get the killer to tip his hand and get this over with. Let the guys catch him."

"Or her," Nita said and Rose nodded.

"That isn't all Daddy isn't going to like," Rose said. She studied Nita and knew she could confide in her sister. "Nita, Tom is the father of my baby."

"Oh, my word." As Nita stared in silence, Rose wondered what was going through her sister's mind.

"Does Tom know about the baby?"

"Yes. And of course Tom's already asked me to marry him—as I predicted he would," Rose replied, glancing at her sister while she stirred her chocolate and milk. The spoon clinked against the glass in the quiet kitchen. "I declined his offer."

"Oh, Rose. Are you sure about your refusal? Are you really thinking this through?"

"Absolutely. He didn't propose because of his undying love for me. Nita, you would have done the same and you know it." Rose looked at Nita questioningly. "Want a cookie and pop?"

"Sure. I'll take you up on that," Nita said, crossing the kitchen to get a chocolate-chip cookie. She opened the refrigerator, helped herself to a cold bottle of pop and opened it while Rose pulled out a chair and sat at the kitchen table. Nita joined her, sitting facing her. Sunlight spilled through the large windows, and Rose thought it was such a sunny, peaceful day for so much to be happening.

"If I had to make a decision, I think I'd give marriage a chance," Nita said tentatively. "After all, you went out with him last night, so there must be something between the two of you."

"What's between us is a very physical relationship. That's no basis for accepting his proposal that was given for one reason only."

"It's a damned good reason, I'd say," Nita stated solemnly.

"There's got to be more to the relationship than passion. You're friends with Connor."

Nita nodded. "Isn't there a strong chance of you and Tom becoming friends?"

"There might be, but he's bought a ranch and wants to settle out here."

"Oh, damn. That's why you don't want to think about marrying him," Nita said. "I don't understand how you can feel that way when you grew up here. I think this is the most wonderful spot on earth." She shook her head. "Well, there goes any chance of marriage to Tom."

"I'm afraid so."

"You might feel differently about ranch life now that you're grown up," Nita said.

"Whose side are you on?"

"Yours—and maybe your baby's."

"Sorry, Nita," Rose said, instantly contrite that she had snapped at Nita. "I know you'll support me and you're interested in my welfare, not Tom's."

"It's the first time since Mother died that you haven't been able to control things," Nita replied quietly. "That's bound to be upsetting."

Rose tried to smile. "That's an understatement. I know I have to tell Daddy, but damn, I hate to. A Devlin and a Windcroft making a baby."

"Just tell him. He won't care because the only thing on his mind is that he will become a grandfather. Rose, I've never seen him like this. He's overjoyed and hums and sings all day if he isn't talking about building you a nursery."

"This isn't what he wanted when he longed for a grandchild and you know it."

"It'll be all right," Nita insisted. "You'll see. Tell Daddy the truth about Tom and let him get used to the idea. If it turns out that it really wasn't the Devlins causing us trouble, he might even like Tom. Speaking of Tom—I thought the plan was for him to stay with you 24/7. I don't see any evidence of him around here."

"He's gone home to pack. Tomorrow we'll circulate the rumor that I know the location of the treasure."

"I hope this works. At least since the Devlins have started helping patrol the ranch, we haven't had another incident." With a scrape of her boots on the terra-cotta floor, Nita stood and headed toward the door. "I gotta go." She paused to look back at Rose. "Cheer up. It ought to be better now."

"I don't know where you get that."

"It will. You'll see. I promised I'd be there with Jimmy when they unload the sorrel we're getting today. Want to come with me?"

"I'll pass on that," Rose replied. "Thanks, Nita, for coming to see me."

"Sure," Nita replied cheerfully as Rose walked to the door with her.

Aware that Tom would be back in a few hours, Rose closed the door and returned to the kitchen with her thoughts on Tom.

His marriage proposal was exactly what she had predicted from him. Well, no way. She wanted a love match, not a husband who felt duty bound to marry her.

As soon as she gave birth, Rose knew that Jane and her father were going to want her to stay at the farm permanently so they could help raise her baby. That wasn't what Rose wanted to do either. She would live here until her baby was born, but later, she wanted to return to Dallas and not be buried out in the country in West Texas. For too long this was what she had struggled to get away from.

She finished her milk, then went to her office to work. An hour later she turned off her computer because she couldn't keep her mind off Tom and on her work.

She decided to get ready for the evening and facing Tom again. She recalled the long, hard look he had given her before he'd left. What was he feeling now?

Tom returned home to shower and pack.

As he tossed clothes into a suitcase, he thought about the future. He hadn't intended for a pregnancy to happen and neither had Rose.

This wasn't what he had dreamed about—far from it. He and Rose did not have a loving and trusting relationship. But they were going to have a baby. The wonder of becoming a father took Tom's breath. A little girl. He didn't know a thing about baby girls, but he would learn.

Hurt tinged with anger smoldered when he thought about Rose keeping the truth from him. Yet in fairness, what could he expect when he hadn't made a commitment to her? He hadn't even looked her up after their first incredible night together.

Now he understood why she had had such an intense reaction to seeing him yesterday—the first time since Houston. And the first time here at her own home place. No wonder her jaw had dropped and she'd looked stunned.

The thought of his marriage proposal raised questions and qualms. Was he really ready for marriage? Would he fall in love with Rose? On a purely physical level she appealed to him more than any other woman he had ever known.

"Dammit!" he said aloud. He was willing to marry and try to establish a family for the sake of the baby. At the same time, he wanted to become a rancher, and being the wife of a rancher was the last thing Rose wanted. He paused to think about the land he had purchased. Rose was strong-willed, had her own business, knew what she wanted in life.

To himself he vowed that whatever happened, he would do everything in his power to keep from hurting their baby.

Shortly after six o'clock he left for the horse farm. His emotions were stormy and fears for Rose's safety plagued him. The Club's plan to use her to lure the killer out of hiding still felt wrong. Common sense told him that she would have plenty of protection, but he knew how things could go awry so quickly with the best of plans. He didn't know if his worries had heightened because of Connor's opposition to the plan or if he truly had a premonition of disaster.

It was half past seven when Rose heard Tom's pickup and she went to the back door to greet him. He carried grocery sacks in both arms. Dressed in jeans, a blue shirt and boots, he was as handsome as ever, and she tried to ignore the inevitable jump in her pulse. Why did she have this intense reaction to him? Why did he look more handsome to her than every other man? Why couldn't she see him without this leap in her heartbeat?

Was it purely physical attraction? Or was it deeper than that? She had too many unanswered questions that plagued her. He brushed past her and set the sacks on the island in the kitchen. She helped him unload the groceries, catching a scent of his enticing aftershave. While they prepared dinner and made casual conversation, she was conscious of him moving around near her. Each occasional contact between them stirred more tingles.

They ate in the cozy kitchen with a fire roaring in the

fireplace. Over dinner Tom studied her. "Let me refill your water unless you want tea. Which would you prefer?" he asked.

If the moment hadn't been so solemn, she would have been amused how he had hovered over her since his arrival. "I'll take water," she replied, watching while he refilled their glasses. When their fingers touched, she saw the flicker in the depths of his eyes and knew he experienced the same sparks that she had.

"You look pretty, Rose," he said solemnly, and she wondered if, in spite of his anger, he was planning another seduction. Since she had turned down his proposal, she had to start resisting him physically.

As soon as they finished eating he stood and came around to her, touching her shoulder lightly. "Let's go sit in the family room," he suggested. As they left the kitchen, he glanced down at her. "How have you felt?"

"I'm fine, and have been ninety-five percent of the time," she said.

"That's good to hear. Do you have a doctor in Dallas and one here?"

"I don't have a local obstetrician yet."

"I'm sure Uncle Lucas knows doctors in Royal. I'll help you find one," Tom said.

"I'll find a doctor," she replied, thinking that Tom was trying to take charge of small aspects of her life just as she had suspected he might.

When they sat on the sofa, he moved closer to her, revving her pulse another notch. She should move back, but he touched her shoulder lightly, a mere brush of his fingers. "I'm glad I'm with you, Rose."

She nodded, fighting an inner battle with herself. She wanted to close the space between them and kiss him. At the same time, she wanted to maintain some degree of aloofness.

"It's temporary," she said softly. "You'll be here until the trouble with the farm ends."

They gazed into each other's eyes and tension heightened. "You're not changing, Tom, and I can't change. There isn't a future for us," she said softly.

"We'll share a future—the question is, where and what kind?" He placed both hands on her shoulders and gazed down solemnly.

"I have another question, Rose."

She inhaled, knowing it was something she might not want to answer for him to give her a warning. "What's on your mind?"

"Rose, have you told Will that I'm the father?"

Seven

Guilt swamped Rose again for the way she had handled this situation. She shook her head. "No, I haven't, but I intend to."

"I'll tell him," Tom said firmly, "and let's not argue about it."

"I should tell him first and then you can talk to him. I know I should have let him know before now. Nita already knows. She came to see me after you left today."

"So is some of the old hatred of the Devlins stirring?"

"Never with Nita."

"I guess Connor told her about the plan to lure the killer, didn't he?"

"Yes, and she agrees that it's necessary. She wants to be the decoy, but the only way to get the others to accept Nita would be to announce my pregnancy, and I'm not ready to do that. I don't mind being the bait. I'll be safe with so many people guarding me."

"Rose, I want to talk to your dad soon. In the morning if possible. He needs to know some things."

"I'll tell Daddy you're the father and get it over with," Rose said. "I might as well do it right now. They'll be finished supper and he and Jane will just be sitting reading or watching television."

"I'll go with you," Tom said. "Even if I weren't going to talk to him, I'd accompany you. From now on I'm sticking with you like glue."

"You don't have to stay right with me when all I do is cross the drive to go to the main house."

"Oh, yes, I do. Anytime you step outside this place, I'll be with you. End of discussion."

Rose knew there was no point in arguing with him, so she nodded. "You know when you tell Daddy that you want to marry me, he'll side with you."

"I don't know that, but that's interesting. I'm glad to hear that he's not going to run me off the place with his shotgun. He has more reason now than before."

"I'm as responsible for this pregnancy as you. He can't lay all the blame on you."

"Laying blame doesn't matter," Tom answered. "It's our future that's important, not the past."

"Let me call Nita and tell her we're coming over. I want to talk to Daddy alone."

Tom dropped his hands from her shoulders and waited while she made arrangements with Nita and Connor. When Rose hung up, she got her jacket and joined Tom.

They walked to the house in silence. The sun had gone down, making the air chilly. Tom's hand enveloped hers as they strolled along, a moment suspended in time that made her conscious that, beneath the arguments, a friendship of sorts was developing between them.

She found her father in the living room. "Just wait in the kitchen if you want. I'll come get you after I tell him."

Tom nodded. "We should be doing this together, Rose. I'm sorry we're not and that this announcement isn't going to be the joyous occasion it should be."

Pain squeezed her heart and she turned away. When she glanced back at Tom, he was headed down the hall. Dreading the next few moments, she entered the living room.

Will sat in his big chair with his foot propped on the ottoman. He lowered a newspaper to place it across his lap. "Hi, Rose."

"Daddy, I need to tell you something," she said, crossing the room and shedding her leather jacket. She sat in a chair near him and leaned forward with her elbows on her knees and her hands clasped together.

"I've been waiting for you to tell me," he said gently, and she was startled, unable to imagine that he had guessed what she intended to discuss.

"I want you to know who the father of your grandchild is."

"It's Tom Devlin, isn't it?" Will asked.

Amazed, she stared at him. "Did Nita or Connor tell you?"

Will shook his head. "Nope. One look at the two of you and I knew."

Surprised, she continued to stare. "We're not in love."

Her father gave her a long, hard look. "Are you certain about that, Rose?"

"Yes, I am," she said. "He asked me to marry him, but I'm not going to."

"Why won't you marry him? Tell me again."

"Because I want to marry for love," she said, having a difficult time getting out the words and suspecting an argument was brewing. "You and Mom had a love marriage. So do you and Jane. That's what I want."

"And there isn't love between you and Tom? Could've fooled me, Rose."

"We barely know each other. Tom offered to marry me out of his sense of duty to me and his child."

"Give it time, Rose. If you have a good man who wants to marry you and he's the father of your baby, I'd say you need to think about this one."

"Daddy, you hardly know Tom either, and it just won't work between us. Tom has bought a ranch here. He wants to become a cattle rancher."

"Oh, Rose," Will said, and she hurt because of the disappointment she could hear in her father's voice. "You're like your mother. You never loved it out here. The farm is my lifeblood, and it is for Nita." He ran his fingers over his face and gazed into the distance, and she could see the pain in his eyes.

"Daddy, I'm sorry, but I can't change. And Tom wants this ranch badly. He's already bought the land. It's impossible for me to think about living on a ranch."

Will nodded and in that moment, she felt a knot in her throat. Her father looked older and she noticed wrinkles in his face that she didn't remember from before. She hated to hurt him, but she couldn't change who she was.

"Thanks for being understanding," she said. She was suffocating under the weight of disappointing her father and didn't want to argue with him about marrying Tom. She stood and gathered up her jacket. "Tom wants to see you. Can I tell him to come in now?"

"Sure."

She hurried out of the room, relieved, still surprised that her father had guessed. She found Tom standing in the empty kitchen. He was gazing out a window and turned when she entered the room.

"I told Daddy you wanted to see him," she said.

He brushed past her, pausing a moment to give her a long, questioning look before he went striding down the hall.

It was almost an hour before Tom reappeared and he gazed at her solemnly. "Ready to go to your place?"

She nodded and wondered what had transpired between Tom and her father, but she didn't want to ask about it.

As soon as they were locked in the guesthouse again, they went to the family room, where Tom steered her to the oversize leather sofa and sat close to her, turning to face her while she scooted back into the corner.

"Are we going to spend all our time together arguing about the future?" she asked.

He stretched his long arm across the back of the sofa and caught tendrils of her hair in his hand, toying with the silky locks. The slight tugs stirred more sparks within her. Only a couple of feet separated them. When his gaze lowered to her mouth, she couldn't get her breath.

In spite of all the differences between them, she wanted to kiss him. It was an irresistible temptation, and she fought an inward, silent battle with herself as his eyes, darkened to the gray of storm clouds, showed the desire that blazed in their depths.

"No," she whispered half to herself, her insides heating and her breath coming in gasps. He wanted her, and it was blatant in his expression.

"Rose, give us a chance," he urged. "You want me in bed."

"That goes only so far. It doesn't cover deeper needs."

"I don't think you're really giving me a chance here," he replied, closing the short distance between them and sliding his hand around the back of her head while his mouth covered hers. His lips, then his tongue, engaged in a sensual duel with hers.

Her heart thudded and desire turned hot and heavy, pooling low within her. She wanted him, and he had to know that she did.

She couldn't combat her longing. Drowning in his kiss, she slid her arm around his neck. Dimly she knew he lifted her onto his lap and cradled her against his shoulder while his passionate kiss became demanding. Currents sizzled over her nerves. She moved her hips, twisting in his arms to press more fully against him.

His hand slipped to her breast to stroke her nipple. She moaned with pleasure, tearing away from his kiss. Tingles radiated at his touch.

Winding her fingers in his hair, she kissed him with a desperate need that drummed along her with her pulse. Her thudding heart drowned out all other noises while she ran her hand across his broad shoulder.

"Ah, Tom!" she breathed, hating the problems between them. Whether he was angry with her or not, she wanted him, but this was leading to more complications and more chances he would bend her will to his.

"Tom, I want you to stop," she said, wriggling away and catching his wrist, struggling to get her longings under control.

He raised his head to look into her eyes, his fingers threading in her hair. "I want you, Rose. It's good between us—really good. You can't ignore that."

She knew he was thinking about marriage again and

her desire cooled. What they had was fantastic sex together, but that wasn't what she wanted as a basis for marriage.

She wriggled away, scooting off his lap to get herself together, catching her breath and feeling his gaze steadily on her. His fingers closed around her wrist. When she looked around in surprise, he framed her face with his hands.

"I want you, Rose."

She shook her head. "You want this baby. If you're so determined, let's keep sex out of the equation," she said, certain that he would lose interest in no time. From the little he had told her, he had never had a lasting commitment to anyone. She gathered that he was always the one to walk away—which she could well imagine—and she expected him to lose interest in her soon. There was still the baby that he thought he wanted, but she wondered if he really knew what he wanted.

She scooted back, but she was almost into the corner of the sofa to begin with, so she pushed lightly against his chest. "You can give me a little room here."

He inched away, arching one dark eyebrow. "I disturb you when I'm close?" he asked.

"You know you do." She shook her head to get her hair away from her face. "We need to cool down."

He gave her a smoldering look that only heated her more. She tried to shift her thoughts to something less combustible.

"I know this decoy-and-protection plan is very secretive stuff, but I'm in the middle of it. I have a right to know more about what's going on," she said, trying to bank the flames of desire. "In addition to you, who else will be protecting me?" she asked and listened to him list his five friends.

"My word! I can't possibly be at risk while guarded by the men you're naming," she exclaimed.

"Don't get complacent. You're at high risk," Tom replied, reaching out to nudge up the hem of her skirt and run his fingers in circles on her bare knee. Tingles radiated from his touch and played havoc with her concentration, but she made an effort to focus on their discussion.

"You'll be bored out of your mind here," she said. "I work at my computer most of the day."

"Shut up in the house day and night with you—no way will I be bored," he drawled in a husky voice that was like a brush of velvet. He pushed tendrils of hair away from her face and tucked them behind her ear, running his fingers around to her nape, caressing her. How easy it was for him! She took his hand and returned it to his own knee, but before she could pull away, he twisted his fingers, interlocking them through hers and holding her hand on his warm knee.

"Scared to have me around?" he asked in a seductive voice. "Afraid you can't say no? Or are you afraid you'll fall in love and want to marry me?" He leaned closer while he talked, his gaze pinning her, demanding her answer.

She raised her chin. "Tom, I'll never live on a ranch."

The heated desire reflected in the depths of his eyes cooled, and she wondered what was running through his mind. She couldn't imagine him tossing aside his plans because she didn't like country life. A muscle worked in his jaw and she suspected that she had summed up his feelings accurately.

"I'll have to admit, Rose, I have my heart set on this

ranch. Let me show it to you when this is over and we don't have to be afraid of a sniper."

She rubbed her arms. "Don't even talk about a sniper. As soon as Daddy can get around, there will be no stopping him from going all over the horse farm."

"He can't yet and when the time comes that he starts to get out again, someone will go with him."

"That wouldn't stop a sniper with a high-powered rifle," she answered grimly.

"Don't think about it yet, because there's no immediate cause for worry. Will doesn't go any farther than the porch right now. With Devlins helping patrol around here, we should be able to keep him safe."

"If I stay shut up here, the killer won't be able to get to me."

Tom inhaled deeply. "I keep hoping something will happen to catch the murderer and you won't ever be involved."

"I'm already involved."

"All right—you won't be hurt," he said grimly. "Maybe we'll catch the person soon."

"You don't have any leads, do you?"

"Nothing substantial," he replied and they became silent.

She thought about the danger and the ruse they would attempt. She prayed it would work and this threat to her family would be over soon.

"After this is over, Rose, will you go with me and look at the land I've bought? It won't hurt you to just look."

She shook her head. "I told you before, there's no reason to see it." He gave her a hard look and she shrugged. "You might as well hear the truth. I want love, Tom. Love is two people who can count on each other, who want to be together through thick and through thin, who enjoy each other's company outside of bed, too," she said firmly.

"It's people who get to be friends first and know each other long and well," Rose continued. "I think people should develop a good, close relationship that lasts at least a year before they think about marriage."

"Rose, you can't order life up to fit the specifications you want."

"My mother always said that she rushed into marriage to my father. She said they should have waited more than three months after they met to get married. She loved Daddy, but she hated the horse farm."

"This isn't like your mother's and father's situation. I disagree that a relationship requires a great deal of time. People fall in love instantly and only days pass before they marry and they're happy forever after."

"Name one," Rose countered.

"Uncle Lucas, who thrives on telling the world how he met my aunt Edith when she was engaged to someone else. Within five days she was engaged to Uncle Lucas. A month later they were happily married in a union that lasted for years until she died from heart trouble. It happens, Rose."

"Well, it hasn't happened between us, and you know it."

"I think you're scared to let go and fall in love. You like to be in command of situations and it bothers you when you're not."

Once again she could feel the clash between them. There was a chasm dividing them that would never be bridged.

"Let's go pick a room out for you. I'm sure you came

all prepared to move right in," she said, standing. "You can have your choice of three bedrooms, mine excluded."

"I'll take the one closest to yours," he said, and she glanced up to find him watching her.

"I'll show you your room," she said briskly, trying to keep passion under control.

She entered a bedroom that had hunter-green and beige decor, a king-size bed and a wall of books. She switched on a lamp. "You can have this room. There are towels in the linen closet in the adjoining bathroom."

"Thanks," he said, facing her with his hands on his hips, scrutinizing her in a way that made her pulse beat faster.

"Breakfast is promptly at seven o'clock in the morning in the main house. Don't ever be late for Jane's meals," Rose said, trying to ignore her physical response to him.

"I'll remember. I'm going to the car to get my things. When do you turn on the alarm for this house?"

"Once I'm in for the night, which is after you get back from your car."

"Go on to bed and I'll take care of it," he said. They gazed at each other and desire swirled around them like rising mist. Along with it was an ever-present clash of wills. She turned on her heel and left, her back prickling as she walked away. She closed the door to her room and let out her breath. The day had been emotionally exhausting, and she knew she was in for the battle of her life. It was either marry him or fight him in court for joint custody. She didn't like either choice and all she could hope was to hold him off and let time temper his position.

He thought they could fall in love, and she recognized that they probably could. But he intended to move to his new ranch and she would never want any part of that. They were at an impasse. Unfortunately this living together every hour of each day was dangerous to her heart. She didn't want to fall in love with him and risk settling for a life that would make her miserable.

She rubbed her barely rounded stomach. How complicated her life had already become. And now Tom was only a few feet away. She could be in his arms any time she wanted—awareness of that fact kept her nerves raw and desire a burning ache.

Thinking constantly about Tom, she moved around her bedroom preparing for sleep. Later she lay in the darkness while her thoughts still churned over him and her future and their baby.

The next day Rose arrived at the Royal Diner at noon for her prearranged meeting with Tom. They were about to set the decoy plan in motion.

When she swung open the door to the diner, crisp cold air swept in with her while the tiny bell tinkled over the door. A bluegrass song on the jukebox was a backdrop for a buzz of conversation while the smell of hamburgers filled the air. The lunch crowd packed the diner and people stood waiting for a booth. It was the first time for Rose to see some people since her arrival back in Royal.

She spotted Tom as he slid out of a booth and waved to her. He was wearing jeans and a navy sweater that made his dark looks appear dangerous, more commanding than ever. Threading her way through the crowd, she was aware of his gaze on her while she returned greetings from the locals.

Before she reached their booth, she saw that Tom could not have chosen better. In the booth on one side of theirs was Zelda Mae Whitman, the biggest gossip in Royal. Seated in the other adjoining booth was Malcolm Durmorr.

As Rose passed Zelda Mae and Vita Langston, she said hello. "It's nice to have you back, Rose," Zelda Mae said. Her blue eyes twinkled. "It didn't take you long to meet the new man in town," she said in a lowered voice. "And a Devlin, too!"

"No, I guess it didn't," Rose replied with a smile as she moved toward her own booth.

"Tom, I have something to tell you!" she exclaimed when she greeted him. She knew that would make Zelda Mae perk up her ears.

When Rose slid into her seat and motioned to Tom to be seated, Malcolm Durmorr glanced over his shoulder at her. "Hi, Rose," he said. A degree of repugnance stirred in her because she had never liked Malcolm.

"Hi, Malcolm," she replied while she wondered if he, too, had heard her remark to Tom. Malcolm said a perfunctory hello to Tom before turning away.

"I couldn't wait to see you," Tom told her, giving her a quick kiss, and she knew that kiss would draw even more attention to them and arouse people's curiosity.

"So you look like the cat that swallowed the cream. Or the mouse or whatever it was."

She leaned toward him and lowered her voice, but she whispered loudly enough to be overheard and she knew that Zelda Mae would be listening. "I have the most exciting news possible!" Rose exclaimed with her pulse accelerating. She hoped she was convincing, because she had never tried to trick people before and now lives were at stake.

"So tell me." Tom stated.

"I know where Jessamine Golden's treasure is," she said, leaning closer and lowering her voice, yet still speaking with enough volume that both Malcolm and Zelda Mae could overhear her if they were listening.

"You know the location of the treasure? It really exists?" Tom asked.

"Yes," she said. "I'm sure I do, but I need your help."

"Keep your voice down," Tom said. "We'll talk about it later."

"No one is paying any attention to us."

"Wait until later, Rose," Tom urged as a waitress with golden-blond hair caught up in a ponytail came to their booth. A pin on her pink polyester uniform indicated her name was Valerie.

"Are you ready to order yet?" she asked. Even though she smiled, her periwinkle-blue eyes were shuttered as if hiding her own secrets from the world.

"You want another minute or two?" Tom asked, and Rose shook her head as she looked back at the kitchen and saw the Chicano bodybuilder bustling over a hot grill.

"I can't resist Manny's hamburgers and chocolate shakes," she said to Valerie, who smiled.

"Good choice. Sir?"

"I'll have the same," Tom said and their waitress picked up the menus and left.

"There's your friend, the sheriff," Rose said, watching Gavin O'Neal motion to Valerie, who went to his booth. "I want you to come out to the horse farm soon. And it has to be during daylight."

"I'll try, but I'm tied up this afternoon and tomorrow I need to help my uncle with a project. How about the next day? Let's wait to discuss the details," Tom cautioned again.

"This is Monday. Can you be there Wednesday after lunch?"

"Sure. I'll arrange my schedule."

While they ate lunch, Tom turned on the charm. She introduced him to people who stopped at their table and noticed that he already knew a lot of the locals.

Gretchen Halifax entered the diner and paused briefly at each booth to greet people. Once again, when she reached their booth, her attention was on Tom and she gave Rose only a cursory hello.

"So the truce between the Devlins and Windcrofts is actually working," she said to Tom, glancing briefly at Rose. "At least until another incident out at the Windcroft place. Then the feud will probably resume."

"Relations between the families seem solid so far, Gretchen," Tom said. "How's the campaign coming?"

"I expect to win. Do get out and cast your ballot for me, darling. Remember, Jake Thorne will ruin Royal's economy."

She moved on, chatting with others before returning to join Malcolm Durmorr. Rose's pulse jumped when Malcolm leaned across the table to say something to Gretchen and the two slid out of their booth. Malcolm hurried to the cash register, paid and left with Gretchen.

"They departed in a rush," Rose whispered to Tom.

"Probably had something to discuss," he said with satisfaction in his voice. He smiled at Rose. "How're you feeling?"

She had to laugh as she answered, "Fine. Just the same as I felt when I saw you at breakfast."

He grinned and touched her cheek. "It's good when you smile, Rose."

"I could say the same," she answered, relieved that he was less tense and angry with her.

They chatted while they ate their burgers and drank Manny Reno's chocolate shakes. Finally Tom and Rose left together, strolling out into a brisk, cool November day. While the wind swirled brown leaves along the sidewalk, Tom straightened the collar of her jacket and his warm fingers brushed her throat lightly.

"I think we convinced them," Tom said. "I'm sure that woman behind you was listening."

"I'm sure she was. Zelda Mae has the curiosity of a cat. You did great getting a booth next to Malcolm."

"I tipped that waitress to put me next to him. He eats lunch here almost every day."

"And you had Zelda Mae on the other side of us."

"That was sheer coincidence. I don't know her at all."

"For our purposes, it was great, but Malcolm may have been even better. He sure rushed Gretchen out of there. Maybe it was to tell her what he overheard. Let's hope the right person will fall for your ploy. If Malcolm isn't involved in the trouble, Zelda Mae will have word about the treasure all over town by nightfall."

Tom gazed at her solemnly. "Right now you get back to the farm. I'll be there after a brief meeting with the Cattleman's Club guys. I'll take the long way and make sure no one sees me. Connor is going to follow you home."

She looked around. "Where's Connor?"

"He's parked down the street. You'll have about two blocks on your own and then he'll turn in behind your car."

"Seems silly and unnecessary."

"Humor us," Tom replied. "Here's hoping it all works

and no one sees me. You head home now, Rose," he ordered, and for a minute she stared at him, thinking how easily he took charge even though she knew it was for her protection. She nodded and turned to go to her car. He fell into step beside her and at her car he reached around her to open her door. When he paused, blocking her way, she looked up at him.

"Except for the family, townspeople don't know about your pregnancy, do they?"

"No, they don't. I don't feel up to coping with all the speculation and questions yet."

His eyebrow arched. "There's a way to avoid some of that speculation, you know."

She clamped her lips together. "I'm going home."

"See you at the farm," he said and closed the door as soon as she was behind the wheel.

When she arrived at the farm, she waved at Connor before she drove to the guesthouse. Now that the plan was set in motion, she had work of her own to do.

As prearranged, Tom went to the Texas Cattleman's Club to report on the incident in the diner. All he really wanted to do was keep tabs on Rose.

At the club Tom strode to the reserved private room, greeting the others, shaking hands with Gavin. "I've already heard that Rose thinks she knows the location of the treasure," Gavin said as soon as Tom was seated.

"We expected word to get around but not this fast," Tom said in surprise.

"I think you can thank Zelda Mae and her cell phone," Logan said drily. "That woman knows everyone and she likes to spread news."

"We sat in the booth by her. Malcolm was on the other side of us—I saw to that ahead of time."

"I hope to hell this works," Gavin said.

"I'll be glad when this is over," Tom said, worrying about Rose.

"I imagine by now word is all over town about Rose discovering where the treasure is hidden," Mark Hartman added. "The two of you must have been convincing."

"No reason for anyone to think it's a setup at this point. The main thing to remember is Rose's safety," Tom said.

"You put on a credible show," Logan remarked. "I was there and saw Malcolm and Gretchen hightail it out of the diner."

"There was another thing we mentioned. Rose asked me to help her and I said I couldn't go to the horse farm until Wednesday. Anyone eavesdropping would assume we were talking about getting the treasure, so now we have a time frame that may push the killer into action in the next thirty-six to forty-eight hours," Tom informed them.

"You guys stay alert and where we can keep in touch with each other," Gavin instructed and the others nodded.

"You know Gretchen was working the crowd in the diner. Maybe we ought to have someone out there actively schmoozing the public for you," Tom said, looking at Jake.

Jake shrugged. "I'm campaigning my way. I'm sure Gretchen has a different approach."

"From what I've heard," Mark said, "Malcolm has cheated on her and has someone he slips off and sees in Lubbock."

"That wouldn't surprise me," Gavin remarked.

"Back to the question—what next?" Logan asked.

"I think all of us should be ready for a call from Tom or Connor if they need backup," Gavin said. His words chilled Tom.

"I agree," Logan said. "What else?"

Everyone was silent until Gavin spoke up. "No ideas. Okay, for now we'll see what Tom and Rose's little noontime pretense produces."

"One more thing those of us who live in the city limits need to do," Mark said, "is vote for Jake. Election day is approaching. No one in this room wants Gretchen Halifax for Royal's new mayor. We need to all get out and make sure our families and friends go to the polls. If you aren't eligible to vote, then campaign for Jake."

"Thanks," Jake said with a smile. "If looks could kill, Gretchen would have done me in several weeks ago."

"That witch. She surely will be defeated," Gavin snapped.

"Well, let's all do our part," Mark urged.

The meeting was over and Tom strode outside to his pickup.

"Tom!"

Tom turned to see Earl Finlay from the Royal newspaper rushing toward him.

"Wait up!" Earl implored, catching up with Tom who waited quietly. Earl had interviewed Uncle Lucas, his family and Tom when they were reunited in Royal. Earl was a distant Devlin relation, so the Devlins cooperated with him but only up to a point. He could push the questions until it was tiresome, and in the last interview Lucas had finally sent Earl on his way.

Gasping for breath, Earl blew locks of brown hair out of his eyes while he yanked out a small writing tablet and his pen. His brown gaze focused on Tom. "There's a rumor going around and I want to check it out and see whether it's only that—a rumor—or if it's true. Do you think the Windcrofts know the exact location of Jessamine Golden's treasure?"

"No, I don't," Tom replied swiftly.

"Aw, hell," Earl muttered, looking crestfallen. "I'd hoped I had a scoop. Is the truce still on between the two families?"

"Are you interviewing me, Earl?" Tom snapped.

Earl's face flushed. "I might be a little."

"Yes, there's still a truce," Tom replied. "There's no treasure, that's just a wild rumor, and I need to go," Tom stated.

"One more question. Who do you think has been causing all the trouble at the Windcroft place?"

"If I knew the answer to that, I would have told the sheriff the minute I learned the truth. I'll see you later," Tom said, heading for his pickup again.

"Tom, do you swear that Rose hasn't asked you to help her find the treasure?"

"Stop listening to gossip. You know how things can get blown out of proportion and get a million miles from the truth."

Earl trotted behind Tom, placing his hand on the pickup door when Tom slid inside. "You must have an opinion as to why someone has been trying to hurt the Windcrofts."

"That could be most anything," Tom said. "Someone who wanted to run them off their land or someone who is an enemy of the Windcrofts. Rose turned down a couple of men around this area. Will and Nita Windcroft both have fired hands who worked for them. Any of those people could be disgruntled and want to get even."

"It's always been common knowledge that Rose Windcroft couldn't wait to get away from Royal and their horse farm. Most everyone figured she came back because of her daddy's injury, but maybe that treasure brought her back. Do you think?"

"I think Rose is deeply concerned about her family and the recent mishaps."

"And you're certain that Rose doesn't know one thing about the treasure?" Earl repeated.

"I've answered that question. Goodbye," Tom said, starting the engine. Looking disappointed, Earl moved out of the way and Tom shut the door of his pickup. With his jaw clamped shut, he drove out of the lot. The plan might be the best way to catch the killer, but he couldn't shake his terrible premonition that disaster would befall them.

Before he went to the Windcroft farm, he wanted to go back to the Devlin ranch. Now that he had a family, he wanted to keep them informed about his life, so he intended to tell his uncle how things had gone at the Royal Diner.

When Tom slowed in front of the barn, Uncle Lucas came out. Barrel-chested, gray-eyed, with powerful shoulders, Lucas Devlin was patient, likable and reliable. Dressed in his usual Western shirt and jeans, he strode toward Tom's pickup as Tom climbed out.

"I've already heard from one of the boys who heard from a friend in town that Rose Windcroft knows the location of the treasure."

"Damn. Did everyone get on a cell phone and spread the word while Rose and I were eating lunch? Is there anyone in Royal who doesn't know about this?"

Lucas grinned. "I doubt it. Small towns have a way

of circulating news. To add to that factor is the gold. When money or scandal is involved, word goes with lightning speed. If I wanted to find out, I'm sure I could tell you what Rose was wearing."

"I believe that. As I told you yesterday, this treasure stuff is all a ruse and I'm staying with Rose to protect her."

"I hope it works, and you be sure to take care. If you want any of us to come help, let us know."

"Thanks. I will."

"If you have time right now, I could use a hand over here. I don't want you to get dirty."

"My clothes wash. What can I do?" Tom asked, always glad to pitch in any way he could.

Tom and Lucas lifted long stacks of two-by-fours from a flatbed truck, then Tom went on to the guesthouse to get some more of his things.

While he gathered his belongings, he paused and made a call, arranging to have three dozen red roses delivered to Rose—at the main house, so she wouldn't answer the door when she was alone at her place. The impulse to send flowers surprised him. Did he really want to court her? Was he doing the wrong thing to cajole her into a loveless marriage? Or was he falling in love with her? How important was this ranch he had bought?

It seemed an eternity before darkness fell and he could leave. In his red pickup Tom drove on back roads through several counties en route to the farm house. When he entered the Windcroft property, he pulled off the road and cut his lights, waiting and watching to make certain no one was behind him.

While he sat in silence, he had time to think. Did he really want Rose to marry him? Did he want a loveless marriage? As well as they got along in bed and otherwise, he suspected they might fall in love. He contemplated his feelings, wondering if he was already falling in love with her.

He had to admit that his attitude was colored by the expectation of a baby. A thrill zinged in him every time he thought about the baby, and he wondered how long it would take him to grow blasé about his approaching fatherhood. Becoming a father was fabulous. This might not be the way he'd intended it to happen, but it would be good.

He thought about the ranch that he'd had such high expectations for. He wanted badly to live in the country. Yet Rose had no intention of moving away from a big city, and he was convinced that she would never change her mind. Did he want to give up his latest dream for Rose?

He wondered again how strongly he felt about her. He remembered her laughter, the hot sex. Merely by thinking about her a few seconds, he could get aroused.

If she wasn't pregnant, how would he feel? He did care about her. For the first time in his life he didn't want to walk out on a relationship before it got serious.

If they caught the killer soon, she would go back to Dallas. One thing he knew for certain—he had no intention of getting out of her life or letting her out of his, not as long as she responded to him the way she did.

After a twenty-minute wait, Tom continued along the farm drive. When the lights of the guesthouse came into view, he let out a sigh of relief. He drove to the back and let himself in with the key Rose had given him.

"Rose!" he called as soon as he had punched off the alarm. "Rose!"

No one answered and Tom chilled, standing in the house while silence enveloped him.

Eight

"**R**ose!" Tom called again. He headed to the kitchen moving lightly on his feet, listening for the slightest sound and wishing he had asked Lucas for a gun. Too late for tonight.

Every muscle was tense as Tom stood in the empty kitchen.

Then he noticed a note propped on the kitchen table. He hurried to scan it. Letting out his breath in relief, he tossed aside the paper. Rose was at the main house. He should have thought of that possibility, but panic had gripped him when she hadn't answered his call.

As he jogged across the drive, he tried to stay in shadows as much as possible, even though he knew it was highly unlikely anyone with sinister intentions would get close enough to keep the houses under surveillance. In spite of knowing that, when he crossed the porch and knocked, he felt on display. As soon as the door swung open and he faced Rose, his pulse jumped.

Looking delectable, she had changed into a red skirt and blouse. He wanted to reach for her and pull her into his arms. The past few minutes of finding her house empty had given him a scare. Instead of hugging her, he jammed his hands into his pockets.

"Come in," she said.

"I drove all over three counties to make sure no one was following me," he told her as he entered the house and closed the door.

"Everyone is in the living room," she said. "We've gotten a few calls this afternoon and Earl from the paper called wanting to know if the rumor he'd heard about my knowledge of the location of the treasure was true."

"He quizzed me this afternoon, and of course I denied it, just as I'm sure you did. But no one wants to accept that after overhearing us today."

"You're right. When he asked if I knew the location of the treasure, I told him the truth. I told him that if I knew where the treasure was located, I would have gotten it already and I would have talked to the authorities about it."

"What do you think he believed?"

"That I know where the treasure is," Rose replied. "He asked me if I found the gold, what would I do with it. Would I tell others? Would I go to the law with it? Did I know what the law was on finding buried treasure on our property?"

All the time she talked, Tom couldn't resist touching her. Pulling his hands from his pockets, he toyed with her collar and lightly caressed her nape with his right hand. He ached to hold and kiss her.

Instead when she took his arm, he walked beside her casually as they went to the family room to join the others.

Nita, Will and Connor wanted to rehash the afternoon and hear about the meeting of the Texas Cattleman's Club members. Connor sat with his long, jean-clad legs stretched out. He had his arm around Nita, who was curled up beside him on the sofa. For just a moment Tom envied Connor and his obviously happy marriage. Tom was surprised at himself because it was the first time in his life he had envied a guy because he was married.

Jane sat quietly knitting. Near her, Will was in his big chair with his foot propped on an ottoman, his eyes full of curiosity. "Rose said all went well," Will commented.

"I think Rose was very convincing," Tom replied. "We'll see what the future brings. At the restaurant I told Rose I'd come help her with the treasure on Wednesday afternoon, so something should happen soon."

All the time Tom talked, he was aware of Rose sitting in a chair near him, so close yet so out of reach. He longed to get back to the guesthouse and be alone with her, and it was difficult to keep his mind on the conversation swirling around him.

Finally to his relief, Rose stood and said her goodbyes. In minutes they sauntered into the dark. Tom put his arm around her shoulders.

"I'm glad to be back here and have you beside me."

She laughed. "I'm so protected, I don't know how anyone can do anything to try to get information from me. I think you guys should let me go into town."

"No way!" Tom argued. "You're not doing that."

"Tom, I'm so sheltered here, no one can get to me. And if anyone tries, they'll see that you're around. If I'm bait to lure the killer, then I have to be out there where I can be seen. Tomorrow I'm going to discuss it with Connor and tell him to talk to the others about it if you won't."

"He won't either. He was adamantly opposed to doing this. None of us would consent for you to go into town. Forget it."

"Maybe you'll rethink it when Wednesday comes and nothing has happened. I think you need to get together with your Cattleman's Club guys and think about the next step. I don't expect one thing to happen between now and Wednesday."

"Frankly I hope it doesn't."

"If it doesn't, then you're not one degree closer to solving the mystery," she argued.

Tom unlocked the back door and switched off the alarm, gazing around. "I'd feel better if you'd stay right here and let me check the house."

"Why? We have an alarm and it was turned on."

"I could get in here without setting off the alarm, turn it off, then reset it and hide in the seconds it takes for someone to leave the house. Connor, Gavin, and the others could all do the same."

"You're not former military or a lawman. Where'd you learn about alarms?"

"I worked for an alarm company one summer while I was in college and I have an engineering degree. Alarms aren't that sophisticated unless you get a very expensive system and I doubt if this one is. Until recently, probably no one on the farm locked the doors at night."

"No, we didn't when I was growing up. Why should we have?"

"Now there's a reason." He glanced toward the front of the house. "You stay here and I'll be right back. If you hear a ruckus and I find someone in here, you run first and call Connor second. Just get the hell out."

She nodded, seeing a side to him she hadn't seen before. "You sound like you've done this other times."

He merely shrugged, put his fingers to his lips and left the kitchen. She didn't hear a sound after he left. She wondered if he carried a weapon. She surveyed the kitchen, moving on tiptoe to open the pantry.

Bright light spilled over shelves neatly stacked with staples, canned goods, bottles and jars. She switched off the light and soundlessly closed the door, looking at the door to the hall closet. She crossed the room to open it and see that everything was as it should be.

In minutes Tom came striding back. "Everything's fine. Come in."

"Are you armed?"

"Only with compliments. You looked good enough to be lunch today and even more attractive tonight."

"Thank you," she said laughing. "And thanks for the beautiful roses."

"Sure. Beautiful flowers for a beautiful lady." His fingers closed around her wrist and he drew her to him. "Come here, Rose," he said, his smile vanishing as he held her in his embrace. "It's been way too long since we've kissed."

As her heart thudded, she put her hands on his muscular biceps. She looked up at him. "Tom—"

"Shh," he whispered. "Just kisses." He leaned down, his gaze going to her mouth until his lips covered hers.

While her pulse raced, she wrapped her arms around

his neck and stood on tiptoe to return his fiery kiss. Pressing against his hard length, she poured all her yearning into it, in spite of knowing that every kiss was building a bridge to disaster.

Tom leaned over her, his tongue possessing, touching off flames that sent melting currents in her veins.

"I want you, Rose," he murmured. "I want you back in my bed like we were that first night." Trailing kisses to her ear, he caressed her nape.

She looked into scalding gray eyes that proclaimed his longing as convincingly as his words. "You're trying to seduce and charm me to get me to say yes to your proposal. You can't get my answer through your head. You have the tenacity of a bulldog."

"I just know what I want," he said, his tongue tracing the circle of her ear and sending more tingles dancing. She ached low inside and wanted him. His mouth covered hers again and his tongue went deep into her mouth, stroking her tongue.

"Tom, stop," she said, pushing against him. "You're trying seduction and you want marriage, which would be wonderful if you were in love, but you're not. This is lust and determination to get your way. I don't want to be part of that. I'll say it again—I'm not marrying and settling on a ranch."

"You won't give us a chance together," he accused, a muscle working in his jaw.

"That's because of your motives. You're not doing this because you really want me or—"

"Oh, the hell you say!" he said in a low voice. His eyes were darts of lightning that made her breath catch. He caught her around the waist and hauled her against him as his head came down and his mouth covered hers again. This time, his kiss was full of such blatant desire that she shook.

He kissed her as if she were the only woman on earth and he was on his last day. His fiery, passionate kiss rocked her to her innermost being. His mouth on hers proclaimed that she was his woman, that he desired her more than life itself.

Stunned by his ardor and the white-hot sensuality that left no doubt that he wanted her desperately, she trembled and clung to him and kissed him in return. Her pulse roared, shutting out sound. Her mind had clicked off, and she was running on feeling and passion. Blinding lights exploded behind her closed eyelids while her world spun out of control.

Shaken by the intensity of his need, she was devoured and empowered at the same time, surprised by the depth of the effect she must have on him.

He swung her up and carried her to his bedroom while he continued to kiss her senseless. When he set her on her feet, her need for him was escalating, driven by his caresses as he slid his hand down her back and over her bottom.

"I want you, Rose. And we can have love between us," he said, grinding out the words while his fingers twisted free her buttons and her skirt dropped away. He pushed off her blouse and stepped back to cup her breasts in his large hands, his thumbs circling her nipples and sending heat waves convulsing in her.

He unsnapped her lacy bra and peeled away the black thong she wore, sliding his hands slowly down her legs while he knelt to trace fiery paths across her belly with his mouth.

She gasped, winding her fingers in his thick, short

hair, and then she pulled him up. "Let me kiss you," she said while her fingers tugged at the buttons on his shirt and unbuckled his belt. As soon as the last clothing was shed, she stroked his manhood.

He groaned, framing her face with his hands. "I want you, Rose. You'll be mine. You're fighting something good and lasting."

He kissed away her answer and picked her up to place her on the bed before moving between her legs. With his manhood thick and hard, he entered her slowly.

She wrapped her long legs around him, running her hands over his firm butt and tugging him closer. He withdrew and plunged into her again, moving with deliberation to fill her. While sweat broke out on his forehead and shoulders, Tom fought to keep control so he could drive her wild with need. He wanted her moving beneath him, desiring him. He intended to send her over a brink and see her lose the control that she always had to have. He craved her and he wanted her to yearn for him.

"Tom!" she cried, tugging on his buttocks, running her hands on the backs of his thighs. She nipped his shoulder lightly. When he turned his head, she caught his lower lip in her teeth and then drew her tongue over his lip.

He bent his head closer and gave her another kiss while she ran her hands over his naked body and moved beneath him.

"Tom, love me!" she implored, and his pulse jumped again. Sweat still poured off his body and he struggled to keep from letting go, drawing out her pleasure as long as possible.

"Rose, my love," He ground out the words and then his control was gone. He moved his hips, thrusting hard and fast, filling her while her warm softness enveloped him.

Arching beneath him, she screamed with pleasure. She gasped and climaxed, ecstasy spilling over her as she stroked his back.

"Rose!" He ground out her name and shuddered with his release, pumping into her before he slowed and then languidly moving with her until he rolled over and propped his head on his hand. "Rose, it's fantastic. We're damned fine together."

She started to say something, but he put his finger on her mouth and gave her a look that made her bite back her words. "Shh," he whispered. "Give us a chance. You're not even allowing us an opportunity to love."

"You're a dreamer, Tom."

"No, I'm not, and no one else has ever accused me of being one."

"And you go after what you want like someone driven."

"Stay here with me."

"I am with you and I'm not leaving," she said, finally beginning to catch her breath. She ran her fingers over his smooth, muscled shoulder.

"No, I mean all the time. Before you answer, think about it. I want you with me."

Rose lay in the semidarkness, the only light spilling in from the hall. She gazed into his eyes while she played with locks of his hair that tumbled over his forehead. Dark stubble was beginning to cover his jaw, and she drew her index finger along his chin.

"I want you with me," he repeated.

"Are you doing this to guard me?"

"Hell, no. I can guard you without being in bed with you."

She wondered what it would be like to be married to

him, but then thoughts of his ranch loomed. Moving to the country was a total barrier. "There are so many questions, Tom. We don't know each other really well. But the ranch is a bigger hurdle. I can't stress often enough that I won't compromise on that. I won't live there even part of the time."

He sighed. "I don't know, Rose. I had my heart set on the ranch. I wouldn't have to stay on it all the time, but I'd want to some of the time and I'd want you there with me."

"I can't do it. I don't like staying here now. I miss the city and everything about it. I even miss the traffic. This is too quiet, too dull."

"I've got houses in cities and houses in the country. When this is over, I'll show you where I live when I'm not in Texas."

"I know you said you have several houses. Where do you live most of the time?"

As her fingers combed slowly through his thick black hair, he shrugged a muscled shoulder. "I have a home in San Francisco, an apartment in New York and a home in Colorado. I keep an apartment in Paris and I have a villa on the coast of Spain."

"What kind of life is that for a child? You can't drag a child from place to place."

His eyes narrowed as he studied her. "I don't have to live in those places. I don't even have to work if I don't want to, but I prefer to. Where would you like to live if you had your choice?"

She knew she was doing something dangerous by discussing homes with him when she hadn't changed her mind on marriage, but she had been with him enough now to face the fact that she liked being with him, even aside from the physical attraction. Was she falling in love with him? she wondered. She tangled her fingers in his thick mat of chest hair and felt his heart beating.

"I've never lived anywhere except Texas," she replied. "I used to want to get away. I never felt about the farm like Nita does. Nita is a daddy's girl and has always liked what our father liked. My mother didn't care for the farm, and I guess she influenced me. I couldn't wait to get away, but I never needed to get far and I've come home often. I love my family and appreciate them more than ever. I just wanted city life for my daily routine."

"You can have an urban life with me," he said solemnly. "Whatever metropolis you want."

"You're saying I can part of the time. And part of the time, it would be ranch life, right?"

He raised up on his elbow and gazed down at her, running his finger along her jaw. "I'm thinking about that one," he said so solemnly she was taken aback.

"You're really considering giving up your ranch?" she asked, stunned that he might do such a thing to get her to marry him. "You might regret it later. Especially if love doesn't really blossom between us."

"I think our attraction is on the verge of transforming into love, more so every day we're together," he replied. He lay back beside her and pulled her close, and she wondered what was running through his mind. She couldn't believe he would give up his ranch—not someone as strong-willed as Tom—but he sounded as if that was exactly what he was considering.

Some of the barriers around her heart fell away, and she kept her own silence, contemplating a future with

Tom, acknowledging that she wanted him more every day she was with him.

After a time she thought about the rumor they had started. "Tomorrow ought to be the day the killer makes his or her move, don't you think?"

"Probably. It'll be before Wednesday afternoon," Tom replied. "One thing I know for certain—you're in a lot of danger. I don't know any more about what will happen than you do, but the killer can't be far away. And everyone in the county wants to believe in a hidden treasure."

"Daddy thinks it really is here on the horse farm."

"So does the killer," Tom replied. They were both quiet for a time, taking comfort from their embrace. "Ah, Rose, this is great," he said, turning and pulling her close against him. "Move in with me. It'll be better than you ever imagined. Give us a chance."

Without answering, she lavished kisses across his chest, but she gave consideration to all he had said to her.

As dawn spilled through the windows, she showered and dressed and went to find Tom, who was waiting in the kitchen with coffee before they went to the main house for breakfast.

"I'm ready. We'll still be on time—" Abruptly she broke off her words and placed her hand on her stomach.

"What happened?" he asked, frowning.

She smiled. "I felt the baby move. It's the first time."

Tom looked at her slightly rounded tummy. "Our baby. It's a miracle, and I haven't grown accustomed to it yet."

She took his hand and placed it on her stomach and in seconds she saw his chest expand as he inhaled. His gaze met hers. "Our baby, Rose," he said with so much awe in his voice, she could only stare at him, surprised by the depth of his reaction.

"I thought you'd want to feel the baby move," she said, starting to walk away from him.

He took her arm and turned her to face him, then framed her face with his hands. "A baby is a miracle, and you in my life is another marvel I want."

Her heart thudded as she looked into smoke-colored eyes that held her breathless.

"There's a lot that's good between us, Rose," he reminded her.

"I know there is," she replied, still held by the desire she saw in his expression. Her racing pulse accelerated when he wrapped his hand in her hair and leaned down to kiss her hard. It was another one of his devastating kisses that plundered and demanded her response, that fanned desire to a searing blaze.

In seconds she was melting, returning his kisses, running her fingers through his hair.

He released her so abruptly, it took a moment to catch her breath. She gazed up at him.

"Give it thought, Rose, and give us a chance."

"I am giving it thought." Wriggling out of his embrace, she took his hand. "We'll start even more gossip with my family if we don't show up for breakfast. We've got to run. If you want to see real trouble, just be late for a meal. We have two minutes to get over to the main house."

"Let's get going," he said.

After breakfast they returned to the guesthouse. Tom went outside to get tools from Connor and work on a broken porch rail, while she headed to her computer to work.

Rose saw little of Tom that morning, but they ate lunch together and it turned into a long, leisurely lunch while they talked about a myriad of topics, and she knew the bond between them was growing hour by hour.

That night they lay wrapped in each other's arms again.

"We went through a whole day and most of tonight and nothing's happened," she remarked. "Maybe we all figured wrong about the killer coming after me."

"I have mixed emotions about it," Tom replied, playing with her hair while she drew circles with her finger on his bare chest. "I'm relieved that no one has tried anything. At the same time, there's a bit of disappointment that we haven't tricked the murderer into giving himself away."

"I'd think you'd feel more than a bit of a letdown," she said. "Y'all will have to have another meeting and make different plans. I told you, let me go into town."

"No way. End of discussion." At Rose's silence, Tom said, "I'm not kidding, Rose. Neither Connor nor I will agree to you going into town now."

"I can't stay here indefinitely," she said, propping her head on her hand to look down at him. "I'll be more of a target if I'm out of the house."

"I can stay here forever," he said in a husky voice, trailing his fingers along her throat. She lay down again beside him and he pulled her close.

His bare legs were entangled with hers and he turned on his side, combing his fingers through her hair. Contented, she gazed up at him while she ran her index finger along his firm jaw and felt the stubble on his chin.

"You're a very handsome man, Tom Devlin. But then, you've probably been told that too many times before."

Grinning, he trailed kisses across her temple. "If so,

I don't remember. It wasn't important until now, but I'm glad you think so." He raised his head. "You're beautiful, Rose."

"Sweet talk. Seductive words," she said, only half teasing. She wondered how sincere he was and how much he did or said something to get what he wanted from her.

Suddenly a flash of brilliant yellow light illuminated the windows and the room. Shattering the quiet, a window-rattling, earth-shaking explosion rocked them.

Rose gasped with shock. As she sat up, fear for her family gripped her.

"That's dynamite!" Tom rolled out of bed and tugged on his jeans.

Nine

Flickering orange light danced over the guesthouse, and Rose's heart plunged, turning to ice when she rushed to the window to see a stable burning. "The horses!" she cried, snatching up her clothes.

Tom grabbed her arm roughly, stopping her. "Don't go out there," he ordered.

"I have to!" she cried. "I want to call Nita and see if they're all right."

"Yeah, but first call the fire department while I phone Gavin," he said. "You're not going to fight the fire or get away from this house. Using you for bait may have worked all too well."

Startled, she stared at him. "I didn't even think of that."

"I damn well did. I think our killer has made his move."

"What good will a burning stable do him?" As quickly as she had the words out of her mouth, she knew her answer. "It gets you away from me."

"It gets everyone on the place away from you. Rose, you stay right here and get Jane to come watch the fire with you. Or if your Dad's out by the stable, you go up to the main house with Jane, okay?"

"Our stable is on fire—"

"You're pregnant. You can't fight the fire, and the most dangerous thing you can do is stand outside, alone and in the dark."

"You're right," she said. Frowning, she seized the phone to call the county volunteer firefighters to help.

Tom yanked on the rest of his clothes swiftly, and the moment she replaced the receiver, he turned to her. "Promise me that you'll either stay here with Jane or be up at the main house with her. Otherwise, I can't go help at the fire. I'm not leaving you here alone."

"I promise," she said, knowing that he was right. "Don't worry about me. I'll call Jane right now."

"Good," Tom said and turned to run out of the room.

Before calling Jane, Rose dressed quickly, pulling on expandable jeans and a T-shirt. As soon as she slipped on shoes, she called the main house, hoping to get any of them. Connor would already be outside and her daddy might be trailing out after Connor. She couldn't get an answer, but as she replaced the receiver, the phone rang and Rose saw that it was from her father's cell phone.

She answered to hear Jane's concerned voice. "Nita and Connor have gone to the fire," Jane said. "I've been trying to call you, but your line was busy. Are you all right?"

"I'm fine. I've been trying to phone you."

"Don't you go help, honey. You stay away from the stable. Will said there weren't any horses in this one tonight, so don't worry. Everybody in the county will be here soon to help. They can get along without you."

"I'm not going," Rose said. "I promise. I'll come watch the fire with you. I figure Daddy hobbled out there. Or is he staying in the house?"

"That's one reason I've been trying to call you. Now don't you get worried. He went out to look and fell over a hose."

"Oh, no!" Rose felt caught in a nightmare and wished she could wake up and the trouble would vanish. "How is he?"

"He insists that he's okay. I think he is, but Connor got him into the pickup and I'm taking him to the hospital emergency."

"You're sure he's all right?" Rose asked, worry for her father's welfare wiping out concern about the fire. "You're not just telling me that so I won't fret, are you?"

"I promise you, I'm not just saying that. You can talk to him yourself."

"Hi, Rose," Will said. "I'm fine and I don't know why all the fuss or Jane's insistence on taking me to the emergency. I need to be at the fire, but everyone got in a dither over my fall."

"I'm glad you're going to get your leg checked," Rose said, relieved to hear her father's strong voice and certain he was telling her the truth. "Please call me from the hospital when you've talked to the doctor and let me know how you are."

"I can tell you right now that I'm fine. If I'd done anything to hurt my leg, I'd be in pain galore. You stay at the house and away from the fire. I don't want to have to worry about you all the time I'm gone. Tom's with you, isn't he?"

"No, he went to the fire because he thought I'd go to the house with you and Jane."

"Dammit, we'll come back home."

"Daddy, I promise you, I'm all right. I'm staying at our house and no one is far from me. I'll lock myself in and switch on the alarm. I want you to go to the emergency.

"You lock up, Rose. This fire may not be an accident."

"Daddy, let me talk to Jane for just a second, please."

"Here she is," Will said and then Jane said hello again.

"Jane, do you need me to meet you at the hospital in Royal?"

"Not at all," Jane replied firmly. "But what about you? We thought Tom would be with you."

"He expected me to go to the house with you and Daddy, but I promise you, I'll stay inside," she said, repeating what she had told her father.

"Your daddy wants me to turn the car around and come back."

"Jane, if Daddy has injured his leg, it won't heal right. You take him to the hospital."

"All right, but you take care."

"I will. Please call and let me know how he is when you find out."

"We will. Now don't worry about us."

"You both take care." Rose broke the connection. She locked the house, switched on the alarm and tried to find a window where she could watch what was happening.

After twenty minutes she wanted to go out on the porch where she could see better. She thought she would go look for just a few minutes and then she would come back inside.

She stepped out to see bright orange flames shooting high, sparks dancing above the burning stable. A thick column of gray smoke boiled skyward and spread into a dark cloud.

What had exploded? Had someone set the fire or was this an accident? She walked to the end of the porch to peer at the burning building. She could hear shouts and see men running around. There were men tossing water on the fire and a pumper truck was pouring a silver stream of water on the hissing blaze.

The men were dark silhouettes against the brilliance of the flames. When she heard the wild whinny of a horse, she prayed the animals were safe. All the lights on the grounds were on.

Standing in the porch light, she gazed beyond the expanse of darkness between the guesthouse and the burning stable.

A horse galloped past. The men would hunt it down tomorrow and bring it back unless it returned on its own. She wondered if they had turned the horses out of the other stables.

Had one of their men unintentionally set the blaze? If the fire wasn't a mischance, who was doing these terrible deeds?

Were these incidents really about the old treasure, which she believed was a myth, a Texas tale handed down through the years?

If that legend motivated these acts, then someone really believed that Jessamine's gold existed and that Rose knew where it was hidden. She shivered and rubbed her arms.

As firefighters battled the blaze, neighbors were arriving to provide more and more help.

This latest deed might again point to the Devlins as suspects. She wondered what her father's feelings toward Tom would be after tonight.

Rose moved to a different place on the porch, where

she had a clear view of the stable. She knew in minutes
they would have to give up on saving the stable and concentrate on keeping the fire from spreading to the adjacent buildings.

Glancing around the yard that was filled with shadows, she realized her new position left her exposed.
How safe was she? Should she go back inside?

She lifted her face to the wind, feeling a slight breeze
that caused another fright. She realized the wind was
blowing the sparks toward the main house. She looked
at the home she loved bathed in bright orange light.

They couldn't let the house burn! Wanting to join
everyone fighting the blaze, she paced the end of the
porch, staring at the fire. She knew Nita would be in the
thick of the struggle. With a catastrophe like the fire,
every hand would help. At the same time, Rose had
promised Tom, Jane and her father that she wouldn't.
She should lock herself inside right now, but she could
see better out here. Only a few more minutes and she'd
go back inside.

Behind her she heard a scrape and turned.

A dark shadow moved across the porch, then a man's
silhouette was black against the brightly lit window as
he ran at her.

Along with men who worked on the farm, Tom and
Connor beat at flames with wet gunnysacks. Nita had
one of the hoses hooked up and was pouring water on
the barn.

Connor's face was a thundercloud, and Tom couldn't
blame him for being angry. Connor knew as well as Tom
did that a bomb had exploded and caused the fire.

With Connor and Tom both living on the farm, with

all the lights and alarms, someone still had managed to get into the barn and plant a bomb. And the person had escaped before the explosion, Tom was certain.

The pumper truck with its big stream of water wasn't stopping the fire that roared and crackled. Heat poured over Tom and smoke made him cough.

Jake was staying well back from the smoke but giving directions because this was his specialty. His profession had been fighting oil-well fires until he'd hurt his lungs too badly to continue to be active.

"Connor!" Jake called, and Tom glanced over his shoulder. "A couple of people should get up to the roof of the house and wet it down. With the wind blowing, a spark may catch the house."

Tom glanced in that direction. At the first threat of fire there, they would have to get the two women out. He had an uneasy feeling about leaving Rose, but he reassured himself that she was with Jane. Rose had promised and she knew she couldn't help out here.

Connor handed his wet sack to one of the men and ran toward the house. To Tom's relief, the wind blew away from the guesthouse.

He knew the Windcrofts had water wells and several spigots outside the stable which gave them water, but the fire was too big now to extinguish with streams of water.

A loud crack startled him. "Get back!" Jake shouted at the men nearby.

Tom rushed a few yards farther from the stable and then turned to watch the last timbers of the roof crash.

While a myriad of sparks shot skyward, flames lapped up the wood. Once again moving closer to the burning stable, Tom beat at the flames and glanced over his shoulder.

"Thank goodness Rose is staying away," Nita said as Tom moved near her.

"One of the firefighters told me that so far no one and no horses have been hurt," Tom said.

"We had the horses out of this stable," Nita said loudly enough to be heard over the roar of the blaze. "Two nights ago would have been a different matter because we had at least six horses in there."

"Watch yourself, Nita. The fire is from an explosion," Tom said. "If you see anything suspicious, let someone know. Don't go in the darkness by yourself."

Nita frowned and Tom clamped his mouth shut.

"We had a small butane tank stored in there," she told him.

Tom didn't answer because it was too difficult to make himself heard, but he knew the explosion was not caused by a small butane tank. Something bigger had created the blast because one end of the stable was completely gone and flames had already engulfed the remaining structure when Tom had arrived on scene.

His muscles ached as he swung the wet gunnysack, but it was a relief to do something physical. Even if the stable was beyond salvation, they had to contain the fire. It was frustrating in every way, impossible to douse, difficult to control—and had started right under their noses. How had anyone gotten that close without someone seeing him? Tom wondered again.

Tom was certain their suspect was a man. A bomb was more of a man's weapon than a woman's, and a man most likely had dug the holes that had tripped Will's horse.

Tom spotted Gavin holding a hose and suspected a lot of club members were trying to help. He knew neighbors were present and he had spoken briefly to his uncle and his cousins.

He looked around the circle of men battling the fire and wondered if the arsonist was among them. Grimly Tom realized that the killer could be in the crowd that was increasing steadily as more and more men came to help. He was tempted to leave and go stay with Rose, but she was with Jane, locked in the house, and as long as the house didn't catch fire, they should be safe.

Tom coughed while heat blasted him in waves and sweat poured off him.

"Nita!" Tom yelled, holding out his sack. "Wet it down and spray that hose on me."

As soon as the cold water washed over him, he turned back to beat at the flames, swinging the sack with all his strength, wishing he had the person who had done this.

His hands ached and smoke filled his lungs. How many hours before they would have the fire under control? he wondered. How long until it was completely doused?

"Tom! Water?" someone asked, and he turned to see the Windcroft foreman, Jimmy Bradley, holding a yellow thermos with paper cups and a trash sack.

Tom filled a cup and gulped the water down, refilling it and drinking half and pouring the other half over his head. "Thanks, Jimmy," he said as he tossed the cup in the trash sack.

While Jimmy turned to move to the next person, Gavin appeared to get water. When the sheriff saw Tom, he walked over to him.

"You better go stay with Rose. The stable's a loss anyway. They're moving to the house and other stables to try to protect them."

"Rose is with Jane. I don't know whether they're in the guesthouse or the main house—"

"She's not with Jane, dammit," Gavin snapped. "Jane left to take Will to the emergency."

"What are you talking about?" Tom asked, turning to ice and tossing down the gunnysack. "I saw Will when I first came out."

"He fell. I helped get him into the pickup so Jane could take him to town."

"Oh, hell!" Tom exclaimed, turning to run for Rose's house without waiting to hear more.

Gavin was right behind him, but Tom didn't pay any attention to the sheriff. Tom's insides knotted and fear gripped him while he prayed Rose was all right. And then, amidst all the other noises of flames and men yelling and hissing water, Tom heard a scream.

Rose's captor spun her around and slapped her hard. Rose cried out as pain burst across her face from his blow.

Even in the dark she had recognized Malcolm Durmorr immediately when he had jumped her on the porch, overpowering her and binding her wrists before she could stop him. None of her screams were heard by the firefighters, and as Malcolm pulled her down the porch steps, she realized that he didn't care if she recognized him. That could only mean that he didn't plan for her to live.

As he hauled her along beside him, she screamed again. He yanked her off her feet, and she would have fallen except he held her up. He turned and slapped her hard with the back of his hand. Pain exploded in her head and spots danced before her eyes.

"Shut up, bitch! If you don't shut your mouth, I'll

beat you to a pulp. You're not getting away, and if anyone tries to rescue you, I'll kill him," Malcolm warned. His whiskey breath was dreadful. "I thought you'd be up there with the others fighting the fire. I couldn't believe it when you stayed behind, but you made it a helluva lot easier for me."

"Let me go, Malcolm!"

He tugged her roughly beside him. "Get going or I'll knock you unconscious and carry you."

With her mind racing, Rose stumbled to keep up. She could feel her face and mouth swelling from blows he had given her. Her eye was getting puffy, but her injuries didn't keep her mind from racing over her dilemma.

She had to do something to get away because she was certain that once he left the farm with her, she would never get back alive. With her hands tied, she couldn't think of anything to do to stop him. He was stronger and had the use of both of his hands.

"Let me go!" she cried.

"Shut up! No one can hear you. Screaming won't bring anyone to your rescue. Now get going or I'll hit you again."

"You know you can't get away with kidnapping me. And if you kill me, you'll get the death penalty."

"They're not going to catch me. No one has any idea now who's been harming the Windcrofts—or that Jonathan Devlin was murdered."

"You killed Jonathan Devlin!" she exclaimed, even though this wasn't new to her. But maybe she could get Malcolm to talk about his crimes.

"I killed Jonathan Devlin, but it will never matter that I've admitted my crime to you."

"That means you plan to kill me, too," she said, still trying to think of anything she could do to stop him.

"You know where Jessamine Golden's treasure of gold is hidden. You reveal your secret to me and you'll make things easier for yourself," he said. "You share the location with me and once I have the treasure, I promise I'll let you go. When I get the gold, I'm leaving the country and I'll release you in a border town."

He pulled her across open land, past mesquite, and Rose was certain with every step she was moving farther from safety and closer to her death at Malcolm's hand.

"You'll never set me free and you know it!" she snapped.

"Yes, I will. You tell me and I'll be so grateful to you, I'll be glad to let you live. And you will tell me, Rose, I can promise you that. You can make it easier on yourself by volunteering the information and not making me force the truth from you."

"I don't know where Jessamine's treasure is," Rose admitted, certain that he would never believe her because he wanted her to know the whereabouts of the gold. She had to escape because she could never give Malcolm what he wanted.

"Rose!"

She heard her name being called from the direction of the house and her heart leaped because she knew it was Tom.

She screamed again as loudly as she could.

Malcolm yanked her around and hit her again. She would have toppled to the ground, but he held her up. "Should've gagged you, you little bitch," he snarled.

He stumbled, and she realized he was having a more difficult time getting over rough ground in the dark than she was. If only she could break free, she might get away from him. She thought he was slightly drunk and she knew he was on unfamiliar territory, whereas she knew every bend and hill and grove on the farm.

Tom was behind her and if she had heard him, he had to have heard her scream. Her hopes skyrocketed that he was following them.

As they lurched along, she tried to jerk free, but Malcolm's grip tightened on her arm painfully. "You're not getting away, Rose. Now move!"

Her fear mushroomed when she saw shiny metal through the branches of a mesquite and realized that Malcolm had a car waiting. In minutes Malcolm would have her in his car on the highway and away from Tom and any hope of help.

When they reached the car, Malcolm yanked open the door on the driver's side and pushed her inside, sliding behind the wheel.

He slammed the door and started the engine, and with every passing second her fear and desperation grew. She couldn't let him take her away from the farm. Malcolm was their killer and he intended to kill her, too.

"Dammit to hell!" he snapped as they pulled away, bouncing over rough, open ground. Her heart jumped because headlights flashed behind them.

She twisted in the seat, looking behind her at a pickup following them. Then she felt the door handle with her fingers and she realized if she could grab the handle, she might have a chance to get away from Malcolm.

Gripping the steering wheel, Tom swore. Beside him, Gavin had drawn his gun.

"You can't fire at him because Rose is with him," Tom said in a tight voice.

The black car skidded, spun and changed direction

to go around a thick grove of oaks. Tom's headlights shone for a few seconds on the driver of the car.

"That's Malcolm Durmorr," Tom snapped.

"I'll be damned!" Gavin exclaimed. "So he is our murderer. You get closer and I'll try to shoot a tire. He's not going fast enough to roll the car." Gavin pulled out his phone, and Tom listened to the sheriff call for help and roadblocks, giving someone instructions and warning them to be careful because Rose Windcroft was in the car with Malcolm Durmorr.

Tom's heart pounded. He wanted to get his hands on Malcolm, but at the moment he was terrified for Rose and their baby.

Mesquite scraped the pickup, and they bounced over the rough ground as Tom sped along.

Determined to get close and to think of some way he could help Rose, Tom decreased the distance between them. His headlights easily picked out the car, and he saw Rose sitting far over on the passenger side. Stronger than his rage was a cold grip of fear.

Why had he left her unprotected? He would never stop feeling guilty over that, yet at the time it had seemed safe to do so because he'd thought she would be with Jane.

The fire had been merely a distraction to give Malcolm access to Rose. If Malcolm had been watching the guesthouse, he would have known immediately that Rose had stayed behind by herself.

"We can't let him get away," Tom said in a tight voice, more to himself than to Gavin. His knuckles were white on the wheel and his heart pounded. "I'm catching him, but I can't ram him because of Rose."

"I'll have a backup in minutes, and we'll have the

roads covered. We'll get him," Gavin replied grimly. "Malcolm doesn't seem bright enough to be the one behind the Windcroft disasters."

"People can get very clever about stealing and coercion," Tom answered, his thoughts only half on the conversation with Gavin. Tom wanted to get his hands on Malcolm once he had Rose safe.

"Gretchen Halifax is close to Malcolm. I wonder if she has any inkling of what Malcolm's been up to," Gavin said.

Tom tried to weave and follow the black car as Malcolm drove erratically. He'd think about Gavin's words later.

Tom prayed that Rose was all right and that Malcolm wouldn't smash the car. At any point out here he could hit a rock and spin out of control. Tom hoped they didn't encounter any of the horses—both for the sake of Rose and the horses. The headlights of his pickup and Malcolm's car cut bright streaks in the darkness, but outside of the light was a blackness that hid trees, rocks and animals, any of which could be disaster for a speeding car.

Suddenly the car door swung open, and to Tom's horror, Rose tumbled out.

Ten

Tom's heart thudded and his breath caught. He sped closer, then slammed on his brakes. "Sorry, Gavin. We have to let Malcolm go while we get Rose."

"I agree. They'll get him on the highway," Gavin said. "Let's see about Rose."

Without waiting for Gavin, Tom jumped out. Feeling desperate, he dashed to her. Sprawled on the ground, she lay still, and his heart pounded with fright for her.

Before he reached her, she stirred, and relief washed through him that she was conscious and able to move.

"Tom," she cried, "Malcolm's escaping. He's the one—"

"To hell with him! Are you all right?" Hot anger washed over him when he saw her bruised face.

"I hurt all over," she said through swollen lips.

Gavin came up as Tom picked Rose up. "Let's get her to a hospital," Tom snapped. He held her close, never wanting to let her go. Fighting the urge to shower kisses on her, he hurried to the pickup.

"I don't think I need to go to a hospital," she mumbled. Tom held her tightly, fury a tight knot along with his fear.

"That damn bastard!" He wanted to pulverize Malcolm for touching Rose.

Gavin opened the door of the pickup, and as gently as possible Tom placed Rose in the passenger seat. Gavin slid into the back. "You can take Rose to the hospital, Tom. When we see a patrol car on the highway, I'll get out to check on Malcolm. With the roadblocks we should be able to pick him up quickly."

"I'd like to see him," Tom said, grinding out the words. The bruises on Rose's face heightened his fury with Malcolm, but he was terrified that she might miscarry because of the tumble out of Malcolm's car. "Do you have a doctor yet, Rose?" he asked her. "I'll call him and he can meet us at the hospital."

"Dr. Reed. Nita found him for me."

"It's Zack Reed," Gavin said. "I know him. I'll call him if you want."

Tom drove as fast as he dared, wanting to get Rose under a doctor's care. At the same time he kept a watchful eye for the black car.

Even though they could see far in the distance, Tom couldn't spot any taillights or any sign of a car.

They reached the highway and Gavin said to turn east. When they rounded a bend in the road, Tom saw the roadblock ahead. "He must have turned the other direction," Gavin said. "Or else cut out across country on the other side of the highway. I'll get out here. Do you need an escort to the hospital to get you there quicker?"

"That would help," Tom answered.

"You don't have to do that," Rose mumbled.

"Don't try to talk," Tom said. "I know it hurts you."

"It's no big deal, Rose, and you can get there sooner," Gavin replied. "Zack said he'll meet you at Royal Memorial."

Lights flashed on three patrol cars, and red-and-white wooden horses were placed across the road, blocking the way. Tom slowed and Gavin climbed out, hurrying to talk to the officers. In minutes two patrolmen moved everything out of Tom's way and one came striding back to Tom's pickup.

"I'll lead the way, sir."

"Thanks. We'll be right behind you."

Even though there wasn't a car in sight on the highway, the patrolman's siren screamed. Tom was thankful for the straight highway that held no traffic.

"This isn't necessary," Rose said.

"How do you feel?"

"Like I fell out of a moving car," she said, trying to smile and then wincing. "My shoulder aches because of how I landed."

"Did he push you out?" Tom asked in a deadly quiet tone.

"No. I got my hands on the door handle and threw myself out. I figured if he escaped with me, he'd kill me."

"You're right. I'm impressed. That was brave and quick thinking. And good to get away from him as long as it didn't injure you or the baby."

"I tried to roll into a ball and protect my stomach and face as much as possible. I honestly don't think I need to see a doctor. Tomorrow if I do, we could go then. And at the speed you're going, once again I think my life may be at risk."

"We've got a police escort and this is getting us to the hospital faster than we could any other way. I'm being careful." He clamped his jaw shut and concentrated on his driving, fear for Rose and the baby making him numb.

"Damn him for hitting you." Tom ground out the words.

"It was Malcolm Durmorr all this time. He killed Jonathan Devlin. He told me."

Tom whipped around to glance at her. "If he admitted that to you, he never intended for you to live."

"No, I'm sure he didn't. He's after Jessamine Golden's treasure."

"That damn treasure."

"Because of his eavesdropping at the diner, Malcolm believed that I knew where the treasure was. I would never have been able to convince him otherwise."

"The fire was just a diversion to get to you," Tom said. "And it worked. I should never have left you alone."

"Who would dream that's why he set the fire? Or that he would risk trying to get me when you and all the others were around. He was surprised I hadn't gone to fight the fire, so he'd intended to kidnap me right under everyone's noses."

"His plan almost worked. That terrifies me. I'll always regret leaving you home unguarded. I should have stayed with you. The stable burned to the ground anyway."

"Stop worrying about it. It's over and I'm here, not in Malcolm's clutches."

"Did he say anything about Gretchen Halifax? I wonder if she has a hint of the double life Malcolm lives," Tom said.

"He didn't mention Gretchen. She probably doesn't

have a clue about what he's up to. But if she does, I hope
Gavin catches her. Malcolm has been cunning enough
up until now to get away with murder, but his greed has
finally tripped him up. Gavin will catch him."

It seemed an eternity before they pulled in to the
emergency drive beneath the Georgian-style portico of
Royal Memorial Hospital. The officer had called ahead,
and medics came rushing out with a gurney. In minutes
Rose was being wheeled into the hospital.

Tom quickly thanked the officer for the escort and
hurried to catch up with Rose. A tall, auburn-haired
aide approached him. She smiled at him. "Mr. Devlin?"

When he nodded, she continued, "Sir, there's a waiting room. Miss Windcroft has already been taken to an
examining room, and Dr. Reed is here to see her. Someone will come get you as soon as you can join her."

"Thanks," Tom replied tersely, moving to a beige
and white waiting room but too on edge to sit down. He
got out his cell phone to call Rose's family, knowing that
once they realized that he and Gavin and Rose were
missing, they would worry. Then he pocketed the phone,
deciding to wait to call her family until he knew about
Rose's condition.

Mulling over his feelings, he paced the floor, stopping to peer out at the deserted parking lot with circles
of light from tall lampposts. Lights burned along the
drive and beneath the portico, and momentarily all was
quiet outside.

When she had gone flying out of the car, his insides
had clenched and, until she had sat up, he hadn't been
able to get his breath.

He had wanted to marry because of their baby and
he felt there was a good chance that he and Rose even-

tually would fall in love. But only a man in love could have had the reactions that he'd had tonight.

He had been in a total panic for her welfare. He couldn't bear to contemplate harm coming to her. He hadn't ever stopped to wonder about telling her good-bye when this was over and he knew he never wanted to say goodbye. He was in love with Rose.

"Mr. Devlin?" a deep voice inquired.

Tom turned to see a tall, brown-haired doctor approaching. "I'm Zack Reed. Rose is bruised and sore and I've given her something so she'll rest better tonight. She'll be fine, but we're keeping her overnight for observation, just to make certain."

"And the baby?"

"Everything seems okay, but I'll look at her again in the morning. They're moving Rose to a room and you can ask at the desk for the room number."

"Thanks for coming to the hospital at this hour."

"Sure. Don't worry. They'll both be fine. She's doing well."

"Thanks," Tom repeated. As soon as the physician left him, Tom went to the desk and got Rose's room number. While he walked down the hall and took the elevator, he pulled out his cell phone and called Connor. In spite of the physician's reassurances, Tom was still worried.

Then Connor answered his cell phone. "Connor, it's Tom," he said.

"Where are you?" Connor asked. "I saw you and Gavin running away. What's the deal? Where's Rose?"

"First of all," Tom replied, "Rose is all right. Just as we suspected it was Malcolm Durmorr. He must've set the fire for a diversion."

"The hell you say! So it really is Malcolm Durmorr. We were right in our suspicions about him. I'll be damned."

"He got Rose, but she escaped."

"Thank God!" Connor exclaimed.

"I didn't know Will hurt his leg. Are Will and Jane back yet?"

"Yes. Will's fine, but they're worried because they haven't been able to get in touch with Rose. I'm glad you called. How'd you catch Malcolm?"

"We didn't. Rose managed to open the car door and throw herself out—"

"Oh, hell! Dammit!"

"She's okay. Malcolm got away when Gavin and I stopped to see about Rose."

"We've got to catch him. Where are you and Rose?"

"At the hospital in Royal, and I've talked to her doctor. They're going to keep her for observation, but the doctor said she'll be all right and the baby is fine."

"Nita will want to come see her as soon as we can get away."

"Y'all can wait until morning because they gave Rose something so she would sleep. What about the fire? Rose will want to know."

"It's under control, thank God! We put it out before any other structures caught fire. The stable is just smoldering ruins that they're watching. Firefighters are still trying to douse small fires when they flare up. Everything's going to be all right here. What about Durmorr now?"

"Gavin had roadblocks and was after him, so they probably have caught him as we are talking."

"I hope so. For all the trouble he's caused, I'd like to get my hands on him."

"I think each one of us would," Tom remarked drily. "I'm going in to see Rose. I'll have her call Nita."

"Thanks, Tom," Connor said, and they broke the connection. Tom paused and knocked lightly on a door.

"Come in," Rose said, her voice drowsy.

He entered the room that was painted the same beige and white as the waiting room. Rose was lying in bed with a small light burning overhead. He ached to just go pull her into his arms and declare his love for her and hold her close all night long. He knew this wasn't the time or place, so he crossed the room in silence.

"I thought you'd be here. I'm not sure I can stay awake long. They gave me something so I can rest better."

He pulled a chair close to the bed. "Don't talk, because I'll bet it hurts you."

She barely nodded.

Her hair was a tangle and her face was swollen. She had a myriad of small cuts and bruises, but even hurt and disheveled she looked good to Tom.

"You don't have to stay with me," she said.

"I'll do what I want," he answered lightly, touching her hand.

"I need to call my family."

"I did, but I'll call again so you can talk to them." She nodded, and he wondered whether she would be awake by the time he finished making the call.

"Did you tell Nita and Daddy?"

"No, I talked to Connor." In seconds Nita answered. "Here," Tom said, handing Rose the phone. He listened while she talked slowly to Nita and then Will before she handed the phone back to Tom.

"She's about asleep," Tom said.

"Thanks for calling us," Will answered. "Nita will be in to see her tomorrow."

"That will be good," Tom said. Rose had closed her eyes and she was breathing deeply and evenly. "I'll stay with Rose. I'm not leaving."

"Thanks, Tom. Thanks for saving her."

"She saved herself, but it was good we were there to get her to the hospital. I hope to hell they have Durmorr by now."

"We haven't heard anything," Will replied. Tom thought that might be bad news, because Connor would be one of the first people Gavin would tell when Malcolm was caught.

Tom told Will goodbye, then stood to stretch his aching muscles. As he did, he saw himself in the mirror and grimaced. He was surprised they hadn't booted him out of the hospital, except they were probably accustomed to people in all sorts of disarray in emergencies. His black hair was tangled; he had smudges of smoke on his face and arms. His T-shirt was ripped and smudged with soot.

He raked his fingers through his hair and then gave it up. He sat beside Rose again.

He longed to hold her, but he was afraid he would hurt her. He moved closer and brushed her hair lightly away from her face with his fingers.

He wanted to marry her.

He stroked her fingers lightly. She responded to him like a woman in love.

"I love you," he declared in the quiet room. He leaned forward to kiss her cheek. When he had seen her tumble from Durmorr's car, his heart had stopped beating. He had been more frightened than any other time in his life. He was going to have to do some real convincing, though, to get her to believe him.

He took her hand gently, slowly closing his fingers around hers. "I love you, Rose," he said again. Even though she couldn't hear him, he liked declaring his love to her. Quietly he sat in the semidarkness, holding her hand until his arm went to sleep. He released her and turned his chair so he could still hold her hand while stretching out his legs and he fell asleep.

Tom stirred and opened his eyes to find Rose watching him. He still held her hand in his and he smiled at her. "Good morning."

"Thank you for saving me," she said and winced.

"You saved yourself. I'm sorry he got to you in the first place. Don't try to talk, because I know it hurts."

"I want to talk to you. Thanks for staying with me through the night."

"I wanted to be with you," he said, glancing down at his soot-covered clothes. "How do you feel?"

"Sleepy and sore but otherwise all right. No cramping."

"Thank heaven."

She squeezed his hand. "I'm glad you're here."

"Rose," he whispered her name, leaning forward. "You can't imagine how much I want to hold you. I won't, because I know it will hurt you, but—"

He never got to finish because a nurse bustled into the room. "We're going for another test," she said cheerfully and Tom stood.

"I'll see you later, Rose." He left and waited through a test and then a visit from the doctor, who finally appeared to tell Tom he could go back and join Rose.

"I can go home," she said.

"Great," he exclaimed, delight making him smile. His worries and fears for her well-being finally fell away. "Rose, that's so good that you're all right and they're releasing you. I'll bring my pickup to the door."

It was another half hour before the hospital personnel helped Rose get into Tom's pickup.

"I'm glad to be out of there," she said as they drove away.

He took her hand and raised it to brush light kisses across her knuckles. "Can you make one more stop at my condo while I get some clean clothes? I keep things both there and on the Devlin ranch."

"I'd like to see your condo."

"Happy to oblige," he replied, and in minutes they passed through the gates in Pine Valley, where he drove to another small gated area of half a dozen elegant one-story condos.

"Come inside and see my place. But I've rarely been here because Uncle Lucas insisted that I stay at the ranch."

She strolled through the kitchen into a living area with a vaulted ceiling, white walls and a polished hardwood floor.

"This is lovely, Tom," she said, looking through glass doors onto a patio that was covered with pots of flowers. "Who takes care of the plants while you're at the ranch?"

"That goes with the condo. I pay someone to keep this clean for me. Can you make yourself comfortable and let me quickly shower? I'm filthy."

"Go ahead. I'll be fine," she replied and sat carefully on the sofa.

In less than half an hour they were back in the truck

and she leaned back against the seat. "Whatever they gave me to sleep hasn't completely worn off," she said.

He held her hand on his knee and wanted to declare his love, but this wasn't the moment to do so. A sunny sky warmed the chilly November air as they sped toward the horse farm.

"I talked to Connor while I was waiting for you this morning. No animals were injured and the fire was contained in the stable, so the building was the extent of the loss."

"Thank goodness! I can't believe Malcolm did all that just to get me."

"If that got him what he wanted, he probably thought it was worth the risk. Look at the other chances he's taken."

When she shuddered, Tom brushed kisses on her hand again. "It's over, Rose. Don't think about it."

The entire drive Tom kept Rose's hand on his knee. "I've got a brochure that's due next Monday," she said. "I need to get back to work, but I know with the fire, Nita and Daddy will need help."

"They'll understand and you're to take it easy today. I heard the doctor tell you specifically to rest, and I'll see to it that you do."

"Oh, you will?" she asked and he glanced at her to see a smile on her face.

"Yes, I will," he said. "You can relax a day."

She turned to look out the window. "All this fight to get our land away from us. That must be what it's all about. Tom, look!" she exclaimed, pointing ahead and leaning forward in the seat.

He gazed down the road and then looked to his left and saw a tangle of wrecked fencing. "Damn, someone tore down part of your fence. Or maybe it was Malcolm getting off the property last night."

Tom slowed, crossed the road and pulled off on the shoulder, sending a cloud of dust spiraling behind him. He eased across the bar ditch. "I want to check it out," he said, getting out of the truck.

As he knelt and studied the dusty ground, he heard Rose climb out behind him.

He stood and gazed all around them. "Judging by the tracks, I think someone has come and gone. This is more than just Malcolm leaving the farm."

"Tom, I see something. Look over there." She pointed and then gasped. "Do you see?" she asked.

"I see three hundred mesquite trees," he said, but then he spotted shiny black metal. "It's a car," he said. "I see it now. Damn. That looks like Malcolm's car. I can't imagine he abandoned it, but there appear to be two sets of tracks, so maybe he had someone waiting for him with another car. Let's go see."

"And if Malcolm is there?"

"He's not going to be parked out here in the boonies on your horse farm, just sitting and waiting for someone to find him. I'll call Gavin and tell him we may have found the car." Tom pulled out his cell phone and talked briefly to Gavin before he broke the connection.

Holding her hand, Tom strode across the rough ground. A few yards from the car he stopped her. "You wait here and let me look inside."

Rose waited in silence while Tom looked in the front window and then the back. He walked around the car. When he circled the front end, he stopped and drew a sharp breath. A body was stretched on the ground.

Eleven

"**G**et back, Rose," Tom called, pulling out his cell phone and calling Gavin again. Curious, Rose followed him and saw black trousers and legs stretched out on the ground. She barely saw the body before she turned away.

While a breeze whipped up dust, Tom called Gavin. "We've found Malcolm Durmorr."

He saw Rose glance again at the body stretched on the ground and shudder. Tom moved between her and the body to partially block her view.

In seconds Tom joined her. "I told Gavin we'd wait because he'll want a statement."

She nodded. "I didn't go close enough. What happened?"

"Someone has pumped him full of lead. He's been shot several times," Tom replied grimly. "There lies our killer."

"So who killed Malcolm?" she asked, mystified.

"Damned if I know. Or why he's here on your land. He had to have left last night, unless he met someone out here and the person shot him because he let you get away. But that doesn't make sense either." Tom raked his fingers through his hair. "I don't have answers. Now we have more questions. I'm calling Connor and letting him know."

She nodded and Tom took her arm. "Let's wait at the car," he suggested, and she moved along beside him while he talked to Connor, then put away his phone.

"Connor and Nita are coming. As soon as they get here, Nita can take you home. I can get Gavin to send one of his deputies to your house to get your statement."

"I'm fine," she said, knowing Tom was worrying about her. "Who would kill Malcolm?" she repeated.

"A man like Malcolm is bound to have a lot of enemies," Tom said, glancing over his shoulder toward the black car. Wind caught Tom's raven locks and blew them across his forehead. He brushed his hair back with his fingers. "Malcolm lived a nefarious life. There are probably a number of suspects for his killer, but why Malcolm was on your land, I can't imagine."

They reached the car and sat inside. Wrapping her arms around herself, Rose shuddered. "I could have been with him—"

"You weren't, so don't think about it. Thanks to your own gutsy moves, you got away from him. Malcolm didn't fare as well."

They fell silent as Rose ran her fingers through her hair and gazed into the distance.

"Here comes Gavin," Tom said.

In the next hour Rose gave her statement to a deputy

and waited with Tom, Nita and Conner while they all watched Gavin walk around the crime scene.

Finally he joined them. "You folks might as well go on home. I'm sure Rose doesn't need to wait out here."

"Any clues as to the killer?" Tom asked, and Gavin shook his head.

"They're checking it out now, but it'll take some time for the lab work." He looked at Tom and Connor. "Malcolm was shot once in the groin and several times in the upper body. It looks like someone was in a rage."

"The kind of life Malcolm led, a lot of people might have been furious with him," Tom said, taking Rose's arm. "If you're through with us, I'm taking Rose home."

"We're going, too," Connor said and Gavin nodded.

"I'll keep you posted," Gavin replied.

"I have to admit, I'm a frazzle," Rose said. "We'll go see Daddy later today, but right now I think I need a nap."

"Take her home," Nita said. "I'll tell Daddy that you're fine. And y'all come to the house for dinner if you feel up to joining us."

They parted and Rose climbed into the truck. "I ache all over," she said. "And I can't keep from wondering who killed Malcolm. Gavin's got a big job ahead of him," she remarked.

"Yep, he does. I'm glad you spotted the downed fence and the car. Someone would have sooner or later, but sooner's better. Let's get you home, where you can recuperate."

"Gladly," she murmured, leaning her head back in the seat. "So we're sort of back to square one—still searching for a killer."

"Except now we know some things, like who killed Jonathan Devlin."

As soon as Tom and Rose were inside her house, he said, "A hot shower will relax you and help those bruises." He placed his hand on her shoulder. "You're beautiful and it's a struggle, but I'll wait until you've recovered before I kiss you. You can't imagine how badly I want to just hold you."

"I couldn't possibly look beautiful today. I'm cut and bruised and pregnant—"

"And absolutely gorgeous. I keep touching you to reassure myself that you're alive. Malcolm got what he deserved."

After a shower Rose climbed into bed. "I'm exhausted," she said. "Whatever they gave me isn't wearing off quickly."

"I promise to be careful, but I want to hold you," he said. He stretched out beside her and with great care drew her as close as he could without pressing against her tightly. "How's that?"

"It's wonderful," she murmured.

"Darlin', I'm going to take care of you the best I possibly can," he said. "I want you to always feel safe with me. I'm not leaving you alone again until they catch the killer. Remember, someone out there still thinks you know where Jessamine Golden's treasure of gold is."

"I don't want to dwell on that now," Rose replied. In minutes she fell asleep in Tom's arms.

The next day after breakfast Rose stayed at the main house with her family while Tom drove into Royal to vote for Jake. He stopped at a jewelry store before he headed back to the horse farm.

That night while Connor and Nita drove to Royal for Jake's watch party, Rose and Tom went to the main house to view the election returns with Will and Jane.

By the time the four of them were seated in the living room, the polls had closed half an hour earlier and both watch parties were in full swing.

Dressed in a stunning red woolen dress that clung to her figure, Gretchen was beaming and talking about victory. In the early count, she had close to the same number of votes as Jake.

"She's hiding her grief over Malcolm well," Rose remarked. Seated on the sofa with Tom beside her and his arm casually across her shoulders, Rose was warm in a bulky navy sweater and navy woolen skirt. Tom played with locks of her hair and she was aware of each little tug.

"Gretchen was hell-bent on this election, from what I saw and heard, but the polls showed Jake leading the entire campaign," Tom said.

"I'm surprised she's doing as well as she is," Jane said, shifting the yellow-and-blue baby blanket she was knitting for Rose's baby.

"Early precincts don't tell the whole story," Will said. "I think Jake will win."

Rose's attention was more on Tom than the television and the election reports and she was glad when after an hour and more precincts had reported, Jake had such a wide margin that the announcers declared a landslide victory for him.

Finally Gretchen conceded in a clipped, brief speech that congratulated Jake. She bit off the words, then turned away from the mike.

"I need to get home," Rose said. "I'm glad Jake won."

"When you're home, listen to the late news and you'll probably hear again about Malcolm," Will said.

"I imagine it's all the old news we heard earlier,"

Rose replied. She and Tom said their good-nights and strolled home.

"I'll be glad to be inside. Out here in the shadows there are too many reminders of last night," Rose said and Tom pulled her closer against his side.

"Believe me, everyone has his guard up and there are more men patrolling now than before."

She glanced up at him. "I can tell that you're watching for someone right now," she said, looking into the darkness beyond the yard lights.

"I'm just being cautious. I can't forget that there is still a killer on the loose and you're still a target."

That night he held her close again until she was asleep and then he slipped out of bed to go through the house one more time. He gazed outside. The grounds were brightly lit all around the house, throwing the area beyond into darkness. He saw Jimmy walking by the stables and knew the men were patrolling the grounds.

Tom had a mental list of things to do the next day and one included getting a gun from his uncle Lucas.

Midday, Tom ordered five dozen red roses for Rose and then took her to stay at the main house while he went into town on an errand. To his relief, she was recovering swiftly from her ordeal and her bruises were turning yellow. Her mouth had already returned to normal.

It was late in the afternoon when he returned to the main house and they all insisted that he and Rose stay for supper.

All the time they ate he kept glancing across the table at her. Wearing a red sweater that clung to her lush breasts, she looked gorgeous, and he longed to be alone with her. All he could think about was getting her home.

The scare they had all had at Malcolm's hands made

Tom want to keep Rose in his sight every second. With all of the others present Tom knew he was being ridiculous, but it was difficult to let go of his fear for her.

After supper, he sat close to Rose, lacing her fingers in his and trying to keep his mind on everyone's conversation while hoping she would soon say it was time to go.

To his relief, they left early in the evening and bundled into heavy jackets. The night was cold and blustery with a storm sweeping in. Tom wrapped his arm around Rose and held her close, watching their surroundings the whole time, and he knew Connor was standing back in the shadows on the porch watching, too.

When Rose and Tom were inside the guesthouse, Tom left to build a fire while Rose made cups of hot chocolate.

In the living room the smell of wood smoke mingled with the scent of the enormous bouquet of red roses. Rose put their cups of steaming chocolate on the coffee table.

She watched Tom as he stoked the fire. His jeans pulled tautly over his muscled legs and his black sweater emphasized his raven hair. She crossed the room to him, and her heart thudded when he turned to look at her.

His gray eyes were filled with unmistakable desire. He could melt her with a look, and she wanted to kiss him as badly as she wanted him to kiss her.

"I've waited all day to be alone again with you," she said, going to him and winding her arms around his neck. While he gazed down at her, he placed his hands on her waist.

"Thank you for the roses," she said. "They're beautiful."

"There are things I've been wanting to tell you," he

said. "It hasn't been the time or place, but your kidnapping was a realization for me." He brushed her hair away from her face and then held her shoulders, and she waited in silence for whatever he had to say to her.

"When I saw you tumble out of the car, I couldn't breathe. My heart stopped and everything in me froze. I was terrified for you."

"And—" she started, but he put his finger on her lips.

"When I was waiting to see you at the hospital, while they checked you over, I had time to think. I realized that I'm in love with you, Rose. Deeply, forever, I'll always love you."

Her heart thudded and she leaned toward him. "Tom!" she exclaimed while her heart missed beats. She started to lean closer to kiss him, but his hands held her away as he gazed solemnly into her eyes.

"Rose, listen to me. I would say this to you if you weren't pregnant."

Surprised, she looked intently at him. "I don't think—"

"Shh. I love you. Period. The end of conversation." As he reached into his pocket and withdrew a small black box, her pulse leaped.

"Hold out your hand," he said.

With her heartbeat racing, she did what he asked. He put the box in her hand. "I want you to marry me, Rose." He framed her face with his hands. "I know now what I want, and it's you forever."

Joy filled her. "This doesn't have anything to do with my pregnancy?"

"Nothing," he said. "I need you in my life always. Don't I act like a man in love?"

"Yes, I guess you do," she admitted.

"I've thought about it and I know what I want."

While her heart raced, she knew the moment had come to make a decision. She looked into his gray eyes and wanted him with all her being. "Yes, I'll marry you! I'll marry you tomorrow if you want!" she cried, pulling his head down to kiss him, seeing the flare of surprise in his gaze that was gone instantly, replaced by scalding need.

The ring box fell from her hands, but she barely noticed dropping it. He pulled her close into his embrace as he leaned over her. His kiss awakened all her senses and set her on fire. In a lifetime she knew she would never get enough of him.

Joy shook her. In a rush she fumbled to loosen his clothing. Urgency tore at her and she wanted to pour out her feelings completely, wanting to love him for hours.

He yanked off his black sweater and then pulled hers over her head. The heat of the flames was warm on her skin but nothing compared to the scalding need that Tom's kisses stirred.

Tracing the bulge of well-sculpted muscles, Rose ran her fingers over his chest before sliding her hands down across his flat stomach. Desiring him more than ever, she swiftly unbuckled his belt and trousers and pushed them away. He stepped out of his socks and shoes and kicked aside his trousers as she eased down his briefs. She inhaled, looking at his male perfection.

"Rose, I love you," he whispered and slipped off her skirt. She stood in the lacy black bra and panties while his hands roamed over her and she tingled all over.

"You're beautiful, Rose," he said, peeling away her undergarments and leaning down to cup her breast and take a nipple in his mouth. His tongue drew hot, lazy circles while his other hand slid over her to caress and torment her.

"Tom, I want you," she cried.

He eased her gently to the floor, kissing and caressing her. His hands floated over her body, touching, an exquisite torment that made her writhe with need and cling to him. She took his manhood in hand to kiss him, stroking him with her tongue until he gasped and pushed her down again, moving between her legs.

As he gazed at her, he looked magnificent, and her heart pounded fiercely. "Come here. I love you," she said and saw something flicker in the depths of his eyes.

"Ah, Rose, you're mine," he said with such desire and satisfaction in his voice, her passion heightened.

He lowered himself, filling her slowly, hot and hard, then withdrawing to thrust slowly into her again. While her pulse roared in her ears, she locked her long legs around him and clutched his firm buttocks to draw him closer, wanting him desperately, finally letting go and loving him without reservations, knowing she was in love.

They moved together and she cried out when her release came.

"I love you, Rose," he said, grinding out the words. Sweat poured off him and he let go, reaching his climax.

She could feel his heart pounding and his breath was as ragged as hers. Joy consumed her that all barriers between them were gone. When she ran her hands over his back, he turned them both and wrapped his arms around her to hold her close.

"I love you now and always," he declared. "I can't say it enough times."

"I think I have a ring around here somewhere, don't I?" she asked and he rolled away and sat up. He lay back down on his side and put a small box on her bare stomach. Then his fingers trailed lightly over her breast.

She caught his hand to kiss him before picking up the black box. Her heart thudded when she raised the lid of the box and looked at a magnificent, sparkling diamond that took her breath.

"Tom, this is gorgeous!"

"It's only a token for what I feel for you. I love you forever, Rose," he said.

She ran her fingers along his jaw. "We don't have to wait. I know I'm in love and I probably have been longer than you have."

"I think I have since that first meeting at the hotel swimming pool."

She wrinkled her nose at him. "I don't believe that. I definitely don't believe in love at first sight—"

"Don't you now?" he quizzed, his gray eyes twinkling as he leaned down to nuzzle her neck.

She laughed and pushed him away slightly. "You'll tickle me."

He took the ring to slide it onto her finger. "I'd like to marry as soon as you're willing."

"We can get married right away. I don't need a big wedding, and with all that's going on right now, a large wedding might be dangerous."

"I know you want to be with your family, but Connor is here to protect them. I'd like to get you away from all this for a couple of weeks."

She thought about two weeks alone with Tom without having to look over her shoulder almost every minute. "That would be wonderful," she said.

"I'll take you any place you want to go."

"I'd prefer to be close enough to get home quickly if

we had to. Too many bad things have happened to be around the world away from everyone."

"Close it is. How about something warm and tropical?"

"Tom, my family," she exclaimed and sat up. "Let's go tell them now! They'll be overjoyed." She began gathering up clothes. He caught her arm and turned her to him while he smiled at her.

"You're not marrying me just to make your family happy, are you?"

Dropping her clothes, she wrapped her arms around his neck and stood on tiptoe. "What do you think?" she asked and then kissed him long and passionately, pouring out all the love and joy she felt.

Epilogue

In the morning on the last Saturday in November, Rose was at their church in Royal. Dressed in a knee-length white silk dress with long sleeves, she bubbled with excitement. As her heart raced with eagerness, she stood in the foyer of the church's small chapel to watch Nita walk down the aisle ahead of her. Nita was dressed in blue silk with blue flowers in her hair. Rose's gaze went to Tom and her heart thudded.

Lucas Devlin stood next to Tom, but her gaze was only on Tom. Wearing a black suit, he looked more handsome today than ever, and she couldn't stop looking at him.

"It's time," Will said to Rose and wrapped her arm in his. She stood on tiptoe to kiss his cheek.

"Thanks, Daddy," she said, feeling close now to both Will and Nita. He smiled at her and patted her hand.

They walked down the aisle together, but she barely knew what was happening or saw anything except Tom. Then Will placed her hand in Tom's and they turned to repeat their vows.

She felt she was drowning in his gray gaze that blazed with love. She suspected she might be glowing with happiness.

Finally they were man and wife. Tom gave her a brief kiss and held her arm as they rushed back up the aisle.

After pictures, they drove to the farm for a reception that was larger than the wedding that had been only for family. The Windcroft house filled with people, and she was separated from Tom, greeted by friends and a constant stream of well-wishers.

"I'm so happy for you," Nita said, hugging her.

"You've been good to me," Rose said, and Nita shrugged away the remark. "Thanks, Nita, for everything you've done."

"Sure. I wanted to do it."

"Nita, I'm sorry for things when we were growing up. I have to admit, I was jealous of you and your relationship with Daddy."

"Forget it, Rose. That was kid stuff. Doesn't matter now."

She looked into Nita's eyes. "Maybe I've grown up some," Rose said. "All of you have been so good to me."

"You'd do the same for me. Stop worrying about the past and enjoy your wedding day."

Rose looked across the crowded living room, trying to spot Tom. Sunlight streamed through the long windows and bouquets of roses and fall flowers gave a sweet scent to the air. Tall and easy to find, Tom stood talking to a group of his friends.

"Rose." When a feminine voice said her name, Rose turned to see petite, blond Christine Thorne, Jake's wife. "You're a beautiful bride," Christine said.

"You are," Melissa Mason joined them.

"Thanks, Melissa," Rose said, smiling at the green-eyed news anchor who had interviewed her about the truce.

"Rose, you look beautiful," Alison Hartman said. Rose greeted the tall, slim woman with lustrous dark brown eyes.

"Thanks, Alli."

"When you get back from your honeymoon, we'll all have to get together," Melissa said. "Course, Alli, you and Nita and Christine see each other fairly often because you've been friends for so long."

"Now with our Texas Cattleman's Club guys so close, I'm sure we'll all see each other more," Nita said.

"Rose, where did you and Tom meet?" Alli asked.

As she related meeting Tom at a business conference, her gaze went across the room again to Tom, who stood talking to his friends, and she longed to be alone with him.

Tom turned his head to look at Rose. He winked at her and a moment was shared when everyone around them was closed out. She pursed her lips as if giving him a kiss and then turned back to the women surrounding her.

Across the room Tom moved restlessly. He wanted to get Rose and leave. Glancing at her again, he thought about when she had appeared to walk down the aisle to him. She had never looked prettier. Her black hair had been shiny and the white silk had clung to her curves and left her long legs bare from the knees down. Her violet eyes had been sparkling and filled with happiness.

Love had blessed them and fulfilled one of his lifelong dreams for a family of his own.

He wanted her to himself and every minute he had to wait seemed forever. He tried to turn his attention to the men around him.

"I'll guard the place while you two are gone," Connor said.

"The others will help if you need them, you know that," Tom said, speaking for his friends and seeing them nod. "After Rose's kidnapping, I want to get her away for a couple of weeks. If you need us back here before that time is up, just call. We can fly right back."

"I think Malcolm's death raised more questions than it solved. Our killer is still out there," Gavin said solemnly. His brown eyes were full of worry and he gazed slowly around the crowd. "I know there's no killer in this bunch, but it must be someone close. It has to be someone who knows the layout of the horse farm."

For a moment all of them were silent. "There are so many people who have been to the farm," Tom said. "People board their horses here or come out to buy a horse. There is a world of people who know the layout."

"That's one of our problems," Gavin said.

"At least you'll get Rose out of danger temporarily," Logan remarked. "There are still people who think she knows the whereabouts of the treasure."

"I'd like to take all that back. I hate to think about her in danger," Tom said. "How I wish we'd never tried that ploy."

"When word gets around everywhere about your marriage, someone might begin to put it together that there wasn't actually an end to the truce," Logan added.

"When you two get back, we should have a party to

celebrate Jake's victory as Royal's new mayor," Mark suggested.

"Let's wait until we catch the killer to celebrate," Jake said. "Thanks, guys, for all the support you gave me. Gretchen barely speaks to me and if looks could kill, I would be done for."

"You beat her in a landslide. She didn't even come close, which serves her right for such a negative campaign," Gavin said. "So now, Mr. Mayor, you have to face the fact that your constituency may hold a killer. We have to catch whoever is behind all the trouble."

"No leads on Malcolm?" Tom asked.

"We're waiting for the results of the lab work," Gavin replied.

"Well, guys, as fascinating as all this is, I'm going to see if I can whisk my bride away from this charming company," Tom said. "See you when we get back."

"He's anxious," Jake teased.

"As if those of you who are newlyweds weren't just as eager to get away," Tom said, grinning and breaking loose from his friends. He turned and crossed the living room, speaking to people, stopping to chat briefly when someone asked him a question.

Rose could see him working his way across the room and she excused herself from the group she was with so she could find Will and Jane.

"I think we're going now and I wanted to tell you two goodbye," she said, giving Jane a hug.

"Take care of yourself. I'm so happy for you," Jane said.

"Thanks, Jane." She turned to Will. "You be careful while I'm gone."

"Don't worry. Jane won't let me out of her sight now unless I'm with Nita or Connor."

COMING NEXT MONTH

#1693 NAME YOUR PRICE—Barbara McCauley
Dynasties: The Ashtons
His family's money and power tore them apart, but will time be
able to heal the wounds of this priceless love?

#1694 TRUST ME—Caroline Cross
Men of Steele
An ex-navy SEAL is in over his head when he has to rescue the
woman who broke his heart years ago.

#1695 A MOST SHOCKING REVELATION—Kristi Gold
Texas Cattleman's Club: The Secret Diary
A sexy sheriff is torn between his duty and his desire for a
woman looking for her own brand of justice.

#1696 A BRIDE BY CHRISTMAS—Joan Elliott Pickart
Is this wedding planner really cursed never to find true love—
or has Mr. Right just not appeared…until now?

#1697 TYCOON TAKES REVENGE—Anna DePalo
An infamous playboy gives a gossip columnist a taste of her own
medicine, but finds that love is far sweeter than revenge.

#1698 TROPHY WIVES—Jan Colley
What will this wounded millionaire find beneath this rich girl's
carefree facade?

SDCNM1105

Trust Me
by Caroline Cross

Imprisoned on a tropical island by a ruthless dictator, aid worker Lilah Cantrell finds that her only hope for rescue is retrieval specialist Dominic Steele—the man who broke her heart years ago. But can she trust him to keep her safe...from him?

On sale
December 2005

Only from Silhouette Books.

eHARLEQUIN.com

The Ultimate Destination for Women's Fiction

For **FREE online reading,** visit
www.eHarlequin.com now and enjoy:

Online Reads
Read **Daily** and **Weekly** chapters from
our Internet-exclusive stories by your
favorite authors.

Interactive Novels
Cast your vote to help decide how these
stories unfold...then stay tuned!

Quick Reads
For shorter romantic reads, try our
collection of Poems, Toasts, & More!

Online Read Library
Miss one of our online reads?
Come here to catch up!

Reading Groups
Discuss, share and rave with other
community members!

For great reading online,
visit www.eHarlequin.com today!

INTONL04R

If you enjoyed what you just read,
then we've got an offer you can't resist!

Take 2 bestselling love stories FREE!

Plus get a FREE surprise gift!

Clip this page and mail it to Silhouette Reader Service™

IN U.S.A.	**IN CANADA**
3010 Walden Ave.	P.O. Box 609
P.O. Box 1867	Fort Erie, Ontario
Buffalo, N.Y. 14240-1867	L2A 5X3

YES! Please send me 2 free Silhouette Desire® novels and my free surprise gift. After receiving them, if I don't wish to receive anymore, I can return the shipping statement marked cancel. If I don't cancel, I will receive 6 brand-new novels every month, before they're available in stores! In the U.S.A., bill me at the bargain price of $3.80 plus 25¢ shipping and handling per book and applicable sales tax, if any*. In Canada, bill me at the bargain price of $4.47 plus 25¢ shipping and handling per book and applicable taxes**. That's the complete price and a savings of at least 10% off the cover prices—what a great deal! I understand that accepting the 2 free books and gift places me under no obligation ever to buy any books. I can always return a shipment and cancel at any time. Even if I never buy another book from Silhouette, the 2 free books and gift are mine to keep forever.

225 SDN DZ9F
326 SDN DZ9G

Name _____ (PLEASE PRINT)

Address _____ Apt.# _____

City _____ State/Prov. _____ Zip/Postal Code _____

Not valid to current Silhouette Desire® subscribers.

Want to try two free books from another series?
Call 1-800-873-8635 or visit www.morefreebooks.com.

* Terms and prices subject to change without notice. Sales tax applicable in N.Y.
** Canadian residents will be charged applicable provincial taxes and GST.
All orders subject to approval. Offer limited to one per household.
® are registered trademarks owned and used by the trademark owner and or its licensee.

DES04R   ©2004 Harlequin Enterprises Limited

A new drama unfolds for
six of the state's wealthiest bachelors.

THE SECRET DIARY

This newest installment concludes with

A MOST SHOCKING REVELATION

by Kristi Gold

(Silhouette Desire, #1695)

Valerie Raines is determined to keep her mission
secret from Sheriff Gavin O'Neal. And that's easier
said than done when she's living in his house.
Especially when he's determined to seduce her!

*Available December 2005
at your favorite retail outlet.*

Visit Silhouette Books at www.eHarlequin.com   SDAMSR1205

moment of her life, but she knew there would be many
more wonderful moments that she would get to share
with him, the man she would love as long as she lived.

* * * * *

She raked her fingers through his black hair. "My handsome husband. You are a sweet-talking charmer, Tom Devlin!"

"Thank heaven you think so and thank heaven we didn't have to wait that year to marry." She laughed as he nuzzled her neck and showered kisses along her throat.

He straightened up to look at her, framing her face with his hands. "You're the most beautiful woman in the world today. You absolutely took my breath when you walked down the aisle."

Rose's heart thudded with his compliments, and the look in his gray eyes left no doubts how badly he wanted her.

"I'm the luckiest man on earth, Rose. I love you."

She wound her arms around his neck and pulled his head down to kiss him long and thoroughly. She raised her head. "Tom, sometime we should start talking about baby names."

"In a few days we will," he said, his fingers twisting loose the small pearl buttons down the back of her dress. "Rose, you've made me the happiest man in the world. Happy and lucky." He raised his head to look at her solemnly. "I have you and our baby."

"I know I'm the happy one. Our own family. And someday, a brother or sister for this baby. We've never talked about that."

"We will—"

"A few days from now!" she finished for him, laughing with him, and then his head came down and he kissed her passionately.

As Rose wound her arms tightly around his neck, happiness coursed through her. This was the happiest

"I'm glad. And I'm glad you're off the crutches," Rose said as Tom walked up and put his arm around her shoulders.

"I'm stealing my bride," he said and leaned forward to brush Jane's cheek with a kiss. "Both of you be careful while we're gone." He shook Will's hand. "We'll keep in touch, sir."

"You two be careful," Will said. "Frankly I'm glad you're getting Rose away from here for a time. Maybe they'll catch the killer before you get back."

"We'll hope so." Tom looked down at her. "Ready?"

"Yes," she said, taking his hand and giving Will and Jane one last smile. As she rushed through the kitchen with Tom and across the back porch, she heard a racket behind them.

"Here everyone comes!" Tom said. "Hurry!" They rushed to his waiting car as guests ran outside to let loose a barrage of balloons. Laughing, Tom sped down the drive.

"Tom, your car's painted Just Married and has a string of balloons and tin cans tied to the back."

"We'll switch cars at the gate. I have another car parked there, and Uncle Lucas will pick this one up."

Tom pulled her as close as he could with a seat belt holding her in place. "At last I'm getting you all to myself."

They drove to the airstrip at Royal and in minutes were on a private plane. It was midafternoon when they landed at Cozumel and drove to the villa on the beach that Tom had rented. The moment they stepped inside the door, he dropped their bags and turned to take her into his arms to kiss her.

"Finally we're alone in our house for this next week and I have you all to myself."